Aleister Crowley's Illustrated Goetia: Sexual Evocation

Other Titles From The Original Falcon Press

By Christopher S. Hyatt, Ph.D.
  Undoing Yourself With Energized Meditation
  Energized Hypnosis (book, audios and videos)
  *Radical Undoing: The Complete Course for Undoing Yourself (audios &
    videos)*
  The Psychopath's Bible: For the Extreme Individual
  Tantra Without Tears
  Dogma Daze
  To Lie Is Human: Not Getting Caught Is Divine

By Christopher S. Hyatt, Ph.D. with Lon Milo DuQuette
  Taboo: Sex, Religion & Magic
  The Enochian World of Aleister Crowley: Enochian Sex Magic

Edited by Christopher S. Hyatt, Ph.D. with contributions by
  Wm. S. Burroughs, Timothy Leary, Robert Anton Wilson et al.
  Rebels & Devils: The Psychology of Liberation

By S. Jason Black and Christopher S. Hyatt, Ph.D.
  Pacts With the Devil: A Chronicle of Sex, Blasphemy & Liberation
  Urban Voodoo: A Beginner's Guide to Afro-Caribbean Magic

By Antero Alli
  Angel Tech: A Modern Shaman's Guide to Reality Selection
  Angel Tech Talk (audios)

By Phil Hine
  Condensed Chaos: An Introduction to Chaos Magick
  Prime Chaos: Adventures in Chaos Magick
  The Pseudonomicon

By Peter J. Carroll
  PsyberMagick
  The Chaos Magick Audios

By Israel Regardie
  The Complete Golden Dawn System of Magic
  What You Should Know About the Golden Dawn
  The Eye in the Triangle
  The Golden Dawn Audios

By Joseph C. Lisiewski, Ph.D.
  Israel Regardie & the Philosopher's Stone
  Kabbalistic Handbook for the Practicing Magician
  Kabbalistic Cycles & the Mastery of Life
  Ceremonial Magic & the Power of Evocation

By Steven Heller
  Monsters & Magical Sticks: There's No Such Thing As Hypnosis?

For the latest on availability and pricing
visit our website at http://originalfalcon.com

Aleister Crowley's Illustrated Goetia:
Sexual Evocation

By
Lon Milo DuQuette and
Christopher S. Hyatt, Ph.D.

Illustrated By
David P. Wilson

THE *Original* FALCON PRESS

TEMPE, ARIZONA, U.S.A.

International Standard Book Number: 978-1-935150-29-9
Library of Congress Catalog Card Number: 91-68244

First Edition 1992
Second Edition 2000
Third Printing 2004
Fourth Printing 2007
Fifth Printing 2009

Cover Art by P. Emerson Williams

The paper used in this publication meets the minimum requirements of the American National Standard for Permanence of Paper for Printed Library Materials Z39.48-1984

Address all inquiries to:
THE ORIGINAL FALCON PRESS
1753 East Broadway Road #101-277
Tempe, AZ 85282 U.S.A.
(or)
PO Box 3540
Silver Springs, NV 89429 U.S.A.
website: http://www.originalfalcon.com
email: info@originalfalcon.com

Acknowledgements

The Authors wish to thank James Kababick, James Wasserman, Douglas James and I. Z. Gilford for their invaluable assistance in the production of this book.

TABLE OF CONTENTS

CHAPTER ONE

The Nature of Evil

𝕿 he purpose of this section is to stimulate, through metaphor and analogy, an understanding of Goetic operations and the concept of Evil. Through metaphor, we can only paint a picture. The shapes and colors can only be realized through meditation on the metaphors and doing the work itself. There is no substitute for the latter, and, while many have not practiced Goetic evocation as classically described, they have evoked "unawares," over and over again, the same powerful forces and demons which have both helped and hindered them.

Like many of you I have "made up" my own rituals and have given my own names to these forces. At times I have given them proper names such as John, my neighbor, when his T.V. is too loud. At other times I have called these forces mother, friend, the system "It" or "me."

Sometimes I have benefited from "calling" these "Names" and sometimes I have suffered. Yet, neither benefit nor pain has caused me to reject the "howlings"[1] and simply seek the comfort of "High Magick" alone. If I stand for anything, it is the acceptance of *everything,* (except, perhaps, for the hypocrisy demonstrated by many magicians and mystics who seek the light by running away from darkness).

---

[1] "Goetia means 'howling'; but is the technical word employed to cover all the operations of that Magick which deals with gross, malignant or unenlightened forces."— Aleister Crowley

Goetia is sometimes thought of as a wild card, something that can get out of control, something which expresses the operator's lower desires to control others and improve his own personal life. And in fact this potential loss of control, this danger, the desire for self improvement and great power is exactly what attracts many people to Goetia while horrifying and repelling others. Many label Goetia as simply evil.

Finding evil is a easy job. Just look at your friend, wife, husband, mother, father or for that matter the "guy" next door. The practice of Goetia is that other guy, something dark, mysterious and powerful, something which tells the world that you are interested in yourself, interested in mastery as well as surrender (see Chapter Two in *Sex Magick, Tantra & Tarot: The Way of the Secret Lover*, The Original Falcon Press, for an explanation of surrender and mastery).

Those who have disowned themselves and fear themselves often consider Goetic practices to be evil of the worst kind. Goetia is often thought of as an invitation to madness, the releasing of devouring and frightful forces. What Goetia is—is the releasing of yourself from your own fears and illusions by direct confrontation. Goetic evocation is an invitation to flirt with the ambiguous relationship of "mind" and "matter." Remember, no one knows the true nature or actions of either and thus all arguments as to the "reality" of Goetic spirits are speculative and open to revision.

The question remains: What is evil? Some experts believe it is the intentional doing of harm without redemption. While this definition might provide these experts with a sense of comfort it provides me with little. It is too easy to play with words and ideas. For example according to this definition, Hitler might not be considered evil since some people believe that without his persecution of the Jews, Israel would not have been founded in the late forties. There is always some "good" which our "cause" and "order" crazed mind can find to rationalize or justify a horrible or unfortunate event.

Evil is an "externalization" and "objectification" of something fearful, horrifying, or different. Evil can be a label for
something as simple as a person or an object that frustrates us.
Evil is pain. Evil is the enemy. Evil is the Gods of other men.
Evil is the night terrors. Evil is the overwhelming feeling of
falling apart. Yet all these images are non-sense. Evil like other
ideas exists because we as humans exist. Nature knows not
Evil, neither Good, nor for that matter Law. These are crea-
tions of the human mind, "explanations" which help us quiet
the "terrors of the night." The human mind requires the belief
in "its" idea of "order" for the sole purposes of the human
mind. Thus the nature of evil is the human mind.

Each of us are full of doubts, frustrations, fears and anxieties.
These demons of the soul are the hidden parts of our self. They
are the disowned self, much like Goetia is the often disowned
part of Magick. We normally don't present our dark side to
others. Rarely, will anyone tell you their weak points let alone
their deepest concerns. It is much easier and frequently less
painful to find darkness outside of oneself.

What I present to the world, or for that matter what anyone
presents, is at best a well-crafted ideal image, something
desired, hoped for, something my brain and culture have
helped create. Our mask is an illusion, a piece of the truth, a
necessary one, but none the less only a piece of the truth.

CLINICAL PSYCHOLOGY AND GOETIA EVOCATION

Psychology, particularly therapeutic psychology, deals with
people's fears and doubts. Psychologists label many of these
fears as pathology. Psychologists have carefully followed in
the foot- steps of the Priest, who in his non-scientific but
simple way labeled these things as evil or demonic possession.
*The average clinical psychologist is no more scientific than the
priest.*

In the depths of the psychotherapeutic cave, the therapist
assists the patient in evoking the rejected and hidden parts of

his psyche. The greatest danger for the therapist, and for the patient, is the therapist's counter-transference. When this counter-transference remains unconscious or gets "out of control," therapy becomes dangerous and ineffective. The complexes (demons) of both the therapist and the patient are mixing in an archaic cauldron. All sorts of dangers are thought to be lurking. Sex becomes a strong possibility; so are violent outbreaks. Remember, these dangers are thought to be a result of the therapist's (the operator) losing control of the contents of his own unconscious processes, idealized fantasies, unfulfilled wishes and disowned attributes. Once this happens, it is believed that both the therapist and patient are adrift on a stormy sea in a sinking lifeboat.

The horrors and fears of counter-transference are so great that many State Laws explicitly prohibit "dual relationships" between therapist and patient.; i.e., the therapist and patient may not become involved in relationships outside the safety of the therapeutic model. Dual relationships are thought of as a crossing of role boundaries between the therapist and patient. It is believed that strict boundaries are necessary between the patient and therapist in order for the patient's cure. This is based on the theory that the patient's disease was caused by the breaking of proper boundaries in childhood.

The psychotherapeutic situation contains boundaries, strict ones set down by law, historical precedent, and theory.

The therapist becomes a mirror for the patient upon which the patient's highest aspirations and ideals as well as his disowned "shadowy" qualities can be projected. It is believed by some that the "working through" of both the "dark" and "ideal" illusions are fundamental to the patient seeing himself as well as others correctly, instead of the images and distorted fantasies originating and fixed in childhood.

The disappointment the patient feels when his illusions are crushed can be overwhelming. When his illusions of the therapist are crushed, his own self-illusions are threatened. The patient is both angry and depressed. If the therapist is a good "operator," he knows how to help the patient "crush" his illusions. He helps the patient free himself from his projections and splits. He knows how to help the patient realize that the therapist has both "good" and "bad" qualities and that these diverse qualities can reside in the same person at the same time. The therapist does not have to be worshipped or rejected. Either/Or is the disease. Once the patient realizes this, he also "knows" that the same truth applies to himself. He is neither his ideal nor his darkness. These obvious realizations, however, cannot occur in a cool and objective way; for resolution to occur it often manifests in the heat, and sometimes exhaustion, of intense emotion. Power and force are necessary, and whether this manifests in extreme feeling or behavior or simply in moods and "neurotic" tests matters little. It matters only that they must manifest themselves, and the operator, by the definition of the situation, must stimulate them and in some way control them. He often stimulates them by breaking a taboo either in fact or by implication. He often teases and bribes the patient to be "naughty."

Sometimes the patient is the operator and the therapist is the receiver. In fact, these roles change, but not in a simple way. The therapist sometimes is "blank"—just receiving from the patient. At other times, the therapist is "active" while the patient receives images and conveys them back to the therapist in disguised forms.

What you have just read may sound contradictory: strict boundaries, deliberate violations of boundaries, the situation itself eliciting tests of boundaries, firm boundaries, fluid boundaries. In some sense it all sounds quite "crazy:" projection, illusion, reality, boundaries, violations of trust freeing a person from the prison of his soul. Yet while sounding strange and often unscientific, if performed properly the desired results can occur. And what again are the desired results? One person helping another achieve what he most desperately wants and at the same time most desperately fears: control over his own life, freedom from devastating and repetitive illusions, freedom from reliving the past over and over again in the present. Real therapy teaches the patient how to embrace the whole of life, rejecting nothing, seeing the limitations of his ideals as well as the utility of his weaknesses. Real therapy teaches the art of violation, the breaking of taboos, opening the gates of both heaven and hell. Real therapy teaches style.

TABOOS

Boundaries can be thought of as taboos. (See *Taboo: Sex, Religion & Magic*, The Original Falcon Press.) Taboos are acts, places and things which no one, except maybe the priest, can touch without punishment. Taboos are "dirty." People who break taboos are thought of as dirty, evil people. Yet, in our society is it not the "dirty" the dark which attracts attention? The garbage collector is highly paid for removing the leftovers of living. The bank clerk who handles hundreds of thousands of "dirty" dollars is paid less than the garbage collector. What is the nature of dirt, the common, which at the same time is valued and despised by so many? Money can do the bidding of anyone who has it. Money itself is only a shared illusion. It has no value except what people give it and it has no power except by what people do with it. The fluidity, malleability and indifference of money gives it a power unlike almost any other power in the world. Money sets boundaries and destroys them. Money itself doesn't care. And in this sense money is similar to the Goetia demons. They will work for anyone who knows how to use them. This is one of the horrors people attribute to Goetic workings. You "don't have to be respectable" for Goetia to work for you. Unlike other magical workings there is no implication that the operator has to be "good" and "holy" to achieve results. This idea in itself violates our model of "right" and "wrong," "just" and "unjust." In the Goetic world like in the real world the "bad" can and do prosper. Thus our belief in the moral order of the Universe appears violated by the simple existence of Spirits who will do the bidding of anyone.

Goetic evocation is the rejected "less respectable" side of magick. It is the work of the garbage collector. But it is also the most intimate side of the magick. It teaches the establishment of boundaries, of testing, of bribing, of lying and deceit. It provides the operator and the receiver with visions, suggestions and insights. It actualizes the hidden, the dark, the greedy, the needy, the powerful and beautiful.

Goetic evocation can be very disappointing, sometimes even horrifying, but it can never be boring. Unlike a child who determines the value of its knowledge by the approval or disapproval of a "higher authority" we learn the value of our Goetic work by the success or failure of our own work. Goetic Spirits are *not* the master of the magician but his servant. We do not rely on the "Spirits" per se to tell us that we did well. Goetia work is more "scientific" than other forms of magick in terms of our ability to measure its effects and, to some extent, replicate our results.

Goetic workings can also be potentiated by the use of hypnosis and sex. Trance and "exhaustion" resulting from sexual ecstasy are perfect methods for preparing the mind to receive more meaningful and powerful information.

In this book on Goetia, we have provided the student with a simple to use text on how to begin and become expert at Goetia evocation. We have included images of the Goetia Spirits, not to limit the student, but to stimulate his or her imagination. We have organized the text in such a way that the student doesn't have to flip through dozens of pages to find what he wants or needs.

Equally important, we have provided a technique for the sexual working of the Goetia Spirits. This is a very powerful and sensual method. I have no doubt that some readers will be terrified and horrified at the potential power these techniques will release. We feel, however, that if you desire to practice magick you should practice it to its fullest. Safeguards have been provided, and the real dangers lie more in the mind than in the use of the methods.

Chapter Two

The Initiated Interpretation of Ceremonial Magick

by Aleister Crowley

𝕴t is loftily amusing to the student of *Magical* literature who is not quite a fool—and rare is such a combination!—to note the criticism directed by the Philistine against the citadel of his science. Truly, since our childhood has ingrained into us not only literal belief in the Bible, but also substantial belief in *Alf Laylah wa Laylah (A Thousand and One Arabian Nights),* and only adolescence can cure us, we are only too liable, in the rush and energy of dawning manhood, to overturn roughly and rashly both these classics, to regard them both on the same level, as interesting documents from the standpoint of folk-lore and anthropology, and as nothing more.

Even when we learn that the Bible, by a profound and minute study of the text, may be forced to yield up Qabalistic arcana of cosmic scope and importance, we are too often slow to apply a similar restorative to the companion volume, even if we are the luck holders of Burton's veritable edition.

To me, then, it remains to raise the *Alf Laylah wa Laylah* into its proper place once more.

I am not concerned to deny the objective reality of all *"magical"* phenomena; if they are illusions, they are at least as real as many unquestioned facts of daily life; and, if we follow Herbert Spencer, they are at least evidence of some cause.[2]

Now, this fact is our base. What is the cause of my illusion of seeing a spirit in the triangle of Art?

Every smatterer, every expert in psychology, will answer: "That cause lies in your brain."

English children *(pace* the Education Act) are taught that the Universe lies in infinite Space; Hindu children, in the Akasa, which is the same thing.

Those Europeans who go a little deeper learn from Fichte, that the phenomenal Universe is the creation of the Ego; Hindus, or Europeans studying under Hindu gurus, are told, that by Akasa is meant the Chitakasa. The Chitakasa is situated in the "Third Eye," i.e., in the brain. By assuming higher dimensions of space, we can assimilate this fact to Realism; but we have no need to take so much trouble.

This being true for the ordinary Universe, that all sense-impressions are dependent on changes in the brain,[3] we must include illusions, which are after all sense-impressions as much as "realities" are, in the class of "phenomena dependent on brain-changes."

Magical phenomena, however, come under a special sub-class, since they are willed, and their cause is the series of "real" phenomena called the operations of ceremonial Magic.

These consist of:
  (1) Sight.
      The circle, square, triangle, vessels, lamps robes, implements, etc.
  (2) Sound.
      The invocations.

---

[2] This, incidentally, is perhaps the greatest argument we possess, pushed to its extreme, against the Advaitist theories.

[3] Thought is a secretion of the brain (Weissmann). Consciousness is a function of the brain (Huxley).

(3) Smell.

    The perfumes.

(4) Taste.

    The Sacraments.

(5) Touch.

    As under (1).

(6) Mind.

    The combination of all these and reflection on their significance.

These unusual impressions (1–5) produce unusual brain-changes; hence their summary (6) is of unusual kind. Its projection back into the apparently phenomenal world is therefore unusual.

Herein then consists the reality of the operations and effects of ceremonial magic,[4] and I conceive that the apology is ample, as far as the "effects" refer only to those phenomena which appear to the magician himself, the appearance of the spirit, his conversation, possible shocks from imprudence, and so on, even to ecstasy on the one hand, and death or madness on the other.

But can any of the effects described in this our book Goetia[5] be obtained, and if so, can you give a rational explanation of the circumstances? Say you so?

I can, and will.

The spirits of the Goetia are portions of the human brain.

Their seals therefore represent (Mr. Spencer's projected cube) methods of stimulating or regulating those particular spots (through the eye).

The names of God are vibrations calculated to establish:

---

[4] Apart from its value in obtaining one pointedness. On this subject the curious may consult my בראשית.

[5] The full text is available from Magickal Childe Publishing, NY, 1991. [Ed.]

(a) General control of the brain. (Establishment of functions relative to the subtle world.)

(b) Control over the brain in detail. (Rank or type of the Spirit.)

(c) Control of one special portion. (Name of the Spirit.)

The perfumes aid this through smell. Usually the perfume will only tend to control a large area; but there is an attribution of perfumes to letters of the alphabet enabling one, by a Qabalistic formula, to spell out the Spirit's name.

I need not enter into more particular discussion of these points; the intelligent reader can easily fill in what is lacking.

If, then, I say, with Solomon:

"The Spirit Cimieries teaches logic," what I mean is:

"Those portions of my brain which subserve the logical faculty may be stimulated and developed by following out the processes called 'The Invocation of Cimieries.' "

And this is a purely materialistic rational statement; it is independent of any objective hierarchy at all. Philosophy has nothing to say; and Science can only suspend judgment, pending a proper and methodical investigation of the facts alleged.

Unfortunately, we cannot stop there. Solomon promises us that we can (1) obtain information; (2) destroy our enemies; (3) understand the voices of nature; (4) obtain treasure; (5) heal diseases, etc. I have taken these five powers at random; considerations of space forbid me to explain all.

(1) Brings up facts from sub-consciousness.

(2) Here we come to an interesting fact. It is curious to note the contrast between the noble means and the apparently vile ends of magical rituals. The latter are disguises for sublime truths. "To destroy our enemies" is to realize the illusion of duality, to excite compassion.

(Ah! Mr. Waite, the world of Magic is a mirror, wherein who sees muck is muck.)

(3) A careful naturalist will understand much from the voices of the animals he has studied long. Even a child knows the difference of a cat's miauling and purring. The faculty may be greatly developed.

(4) Business capacity may be stimulated.

(5) Abnormal states of the body may be corrected, and the involved tissues brought back to tone, in obedience to currents started from the brain.

So for all other phenomena. There is no effect which is truly and necessarily miraculous.

Our Ceremonial Magic fines down, then, to a series of minute, though of course empirical, physiological experiments, and whoso will carry them through intelligently need not fear the result.

I have all the health, and treasure, and logic, I need; I have no time to waste. "There is a lion in the way." For me these practices are useless; but for the benefit of others less fortunate I give them to the world, together with this explanation of, and apology for, them.

I trust that the explanation will enable many students who have hitherto, by a puerile objectivity in their view of the question, obtained no results, to succeed; that the apology may impress upon our scornful men of science that the study of the bacillus should give place to that of the baculum, the little to the great—how great one only realizes when one identifies the wand with the Mahalingam, up which Brahma flew at the rate of 84,000 yojanas a second for 84,000 mahakalpas[6], down which Vishnu flew at the rate of 84,000 croces of yojanas a second for 84,000 crores of mahakalpas—yet neither reached an end.

---

[6] The Phallus of Shiva the Destroyer. It is really identical with the Qabalistic "Middle Pillar" of the "Tree of Life."

But I reach an end.

Boleskine House,
Foyers, N.B.

CHAPTER THREE

The Danger of High Magick

...the Single Supreme Ritual is the attainment of the Knowledge
and Conversation of the Holy Guardian Angel. It is the raising of
the complete man in a vertical straight line.

Any deviation from this line tends to become black magic. Any
other operation is black magic...if the magician needs to perform
any other operation than this, it is only lawful in so far as it is a
necessary preliminary to That One Work.

— Aleister Crowley, *Magick in Theory and Practice*

It is no secret that, to many modern students of esoterica,
Goetia has a decidedly shady reputation. On a scale of
spiritual practices one might find Goetia sandwiched
somewhere between "Pacts with the Devil" and "addiction to
the Ouija board."

This attitude is understandable. After all, Goetia is the intentional conjuration of spiritual beings who are, by definition,
Fallen Angels, Evil Spirits and Demons!

From their infernal abodes these *naughty* Spirits are called
forth to act as personal servants to the Goetic magician to ex-
tend his power and execute his will on Earth. The magician
must be ever vigilant to the wiles of the Spirits. If he is
unskilled or loses control even for an instant, he runs the risk
of being obsessed, possessed or even destroyed. This sounds
uncomfortably like Black Magick.

Such behavior is certainly beneath the altruistic purity of purpose that characterize the quest and disciplines of High Magick

and can serve only to bring out the lowest qualities of the practitioner's character...

So goes the argument against Goetic evocation and, so far as
it goes, it is a point well taken.

Yes, the Spirits in question are of the "infernal" variety. But
exactly what does that mean? If we embrace, for a moment, the
popular nomenclature of *High* Magick, "infernal" relates to the
subconscious stratum of the human psyche. *Spirits* inhabiting
these regions would then be the personifications of powers or
energies that lie buried in our subconscious minds—qualities
of our consciousness that we have disowned. They are *Fallen*
because they have slipped from the conscious control of the
deity—ourselves.

Yes, they are dangerous because while they remain unmas-
tered they can surface unbidden and wreak all the havoc
modern psychology blames on "things hidden in the subconscious mind."

To the charge that such practices bring out the worst qualities
in the magician's character, the Goetic practitioner pleads
"guilty," pointing out that this is precisely the purpose of this
variety of evocation. If these disowned qualities are not
brought forth, identified and controlled, the magician, like the
rest of humanity, is doomed to be at the mercy and the caprice
of his own subconscious *demons,* never being allowed the
opportunity to subdue these denizens of his psychic menagerie.

But are the Spirits of the Goetia simply subjective components of the magician's mind, or is there really an independent
objective quality to their natures? This fundamental question
may never receive a satisfactory answer due to the fact that no
one really understands the nature of "matter." But one thing is
certain: one who has never experienced a Goetic Evocation is
not qualified to voice even the most educated opinion on the
subject. It is one thing to be well-read on a subject; it is quite
another to be part of the subject itself. It is an unfortunate fact
that there are many individuals who make magick their *life*

without making their life *magick*. Even the most talented and brilliant expounders of the Art sometimes lose sight of this and focus instead on historical or technical aspects of the subject to such a degree that they ignore completely its relevance to their daily life and happiness.

In light of this, I feel it would be helpful to relate the circumstances surrounding my first Goetic evocation. I beg the reader's attention to what follows because I feel that it contains many of the major components necessary for a successful Goetic Evocation. (I have omitted the name of my former "magick teacher" as it would be recognized by a great many readers.)

WITH MY BACK AGAINST A WALL

It was 1975 and I had never been so desperate in my life. My decision to end a "successful" fourteen year career in music had been one of life and death—mine. It was either continue a lifestyle that was destroying my health and my relationship with my wife and young son, or risk not being able to support them. I was trained for nothing practical. Even my college education, such as it was, was as a Drama major. The pocket change I was still earning from recording royalties and guitar lessons wasn't enough to feed us let alone pay the rent and the bills. I had no job, no car, no money, no prospects...no hope.

One of the few bright spots that characterized this period was my discovery of the writings of Aleister Crowley and my involvement the disciplines of ceremonial magick.

Since the mid-60's I had been a student of Eastern Mysticism and Western Hermeticism, and my interests had finally brought me into contact with a magical society that I had believed long extinct. I passionately involved myself in this group and subsequently became the student of one of its senior officers.

A charming woman in her fifties, she continually impressed me with what I perceived to be her balanced, logical approach to the subject of magick. Her teacher had been a personal student of Aleister Crowley and had even been a resident at his (in)famous Abbey of Thelema in Cefalu Sicily in the 1920's. I was thrilled to be a link in such an historic magical chain and my spiritual practices became the entire focus of my life. Periodically my teacher reviewed my diaries and we maintained constant correspondence. I also visited her as often as I could.

However, my deteriorating situation on the material plane was a source of major anxiety and the distraction inevitably began to affect my ability to concentrate on my "spiritual" practices.

What was the use of all this study if I couldn't use it in a practical way to improve my life? My teacher cautioned me not to mix my planes. "If you need a job, go out and get a job." she wrote. "Learn to walk before you attempt to run." Performing magick to help get a job was, in her words, "low magick" and would distract from the Great Work that I was pledged to perform.

I could not make it clear to her that I *was* trying to improve my situation by normal means, but I also felt the need to magically "lubricate" the situation. Obviously there was a great stumbling block before me and, after all, didn't the esoteric Wisdom of the Ages teach us to look first in *ourselves* for such obstacles?

I was familiar with *The Lesser Key of Solomon—The Goetia*[7]—and it seemed to me that many of the seventy-two Spirits (if one considered them actual entities, capable of effecting change on the material plane) could provide such help. I wanted to perform a Goetic evocation for the purpose of improving the conditions of my material life.

---

[7] *The Book of the Goetia of Solomon the King Translated into the English Tongue by a Dead Hand and Adorned with Divers Other Matters Germane Delightful to the Wise, the Whole Edited, Verified, Introduced and Commented by Aleister Crowley*—Society for the Propagation of Religious Truth, Boleskine, Foyers, Inverness, Scotland, 1904.

This suggestion to my teacher evoked in her an almost hysterical response. She told me in no uncertain terms that I was not ready to practice any form of Goetic evocation. She stressed that only magicians who had already achieved the highest levels of illumination were qualified to do so. "Once you achieve the Knowledge and Conversation of your Holy Guardian Angel you will see all of this as unnecessary."

But how could I obtain the mental and emotional equilibrium necessary to achieve such lofty spiritual heights while my life remained so screwed up? Is it required by the Gods that illumination comes only to the illuminated?

I did not wish to be disrespectful to her yet I was sensing a real blind spot in our relationship.

When I asked her if *she* had ever performed a Goetic evocation she answered, "Certainly not! That is *Low Magick.*"

CHAPTER FOUR

First Evocation

For for the next nine months I continued my disciplines of "High Magick," rising in the pre-dawn hours for yoga, pranayama and ceremonial work with the pentagram and hexagram rituals. I enjoyed the work very much and kept a detailed magical diary and dream records. I constructed and consecrated my magical weapons, mixed the Holy Oil of Abramelin and memorized the recommended texts. My teacher seemed pleased with my progress.

By the Fall of 1976, my situation in the "real" world had degenerated terribly. I didn't have a car or a telephone and that made job hunting difficult. The temporary positions I did manage to secure were so far away that what little they paid was all but taken up by the expense of getting there.

To say that I was distracted by my anxiety would be a cruel understatement. My self esteem was at an all-time low and I began to entertain thoughts too dark to relate. My back was against the wall.

As a last resort and against my teacher's instructions, I decided to perform a Goetic evocation with the expressed purpose of turning my life around and achieving some level of mastery over my existence. I wrote in my diary, "I must succeed, because the consequences of failure at this point are unthinkable."

I turned my attention to the only Goetic text available to me at that time. I went down the list of the Spirits and their attributes and settled on # 55:

OROBAS

The Fifty-fifth Spirit is Orobas. He is a great
and mighty Prince, appearing at first like a
horse; but after the command of the Exorcist he
puts on the image of a man. His office is to
discover all things past, present, and to come;
also to give Dignities, and Prelacies, and the
favor of friends and of foes. He gives true
answers of divinity, and of the creation of the
world. He is very faithful unto the Exorcist, and
will not allow him to be tempted of any Spirit.
He governs 20 Legions of Spirits.

Orobas seemed ideal for my needs. First I lacked the
"dignity" to properly care for myself and my family. (At the
time I had no idea what "prelacies" meant.) Second, in order to
pull my life together I would need the favor of both friends and
foes. Third, because of my studies, I needed confidence in my
divinatory abilities and a good understanding of the Holy
Qabalah. Finally I needed a Spirit in whom I could trust.
Orobas seemed like the perfect Magical side-kick. Orobas it
would be.

Next I had to come to grips with the Temple set up, equipment and the method of evocation.

The Temple was easy. I could use my son's bedroom (the
only bedroom in our little apartment). Using thin masking tape,
I created a circle about nine feet in diameter on the floor. Upon
the circle I placed the Holy Names; for me these included the
names from the Thelemic Pantheon: Nuit, Hadit, Ra-Hoor
Khuit, Babalon, Therion. I made the Triangle from posterboard
and enclosed it with what I felt were appropriate names
(Thelema, Agape and Abrahadabra).

The equipment was improvised and not at all the glamorous magical accouterments I had always pictured: an inexpensive Indian incense burner smoked in the Triangle near a paper facsimile of the seal of Orobas; I scratched the same figure upon the medallion that hung from my neck (the flip side engraved with the pentagram of Solomon); a cup of water for purification; a candle for consecration; Oil of Abramelin to anoint myself and the Temple, and, of course, my magick book.

I had a real problem with the conjurations as they appeared in *The Lesser Key of Solomon*. I was sure that it would be unnecessary for me to mindlessly parrot the tedious series of conjurations precisely as they are written in the text. The endless intonations are obviously intended to do two things: (1) reinforce the operator's belief that he has a "divine right" to call forth and control the Spirit and (2) put the operator in an altered state of consciousness whereby he can *see* and communicate with the Spirit. I was confident that I could achieve both these states without the tiresome archaic language and the references to Old Testament characters for whom I had neither emotional attachment nor respect.

I resolved to simply perform a thorough banishing, then open the Temple with Crowley's *Preliminary Invocation of the Goetia* (see Chapter Seven), which I had already memorized as part of the ceremonies of the consecration of my magical weapons. Then, "intoxicated" by the Barbarous Words of Evocation, I would simply concentrate upon the Triangle and call forth Orobas *extempore*.

The Charge was to be a simple one. Orobas was to immediately do whatever was necessary to help me gain control over my life. I needed to attain the dignity to safeguard the well being of myself and my wife and child; Orobas was to remain as my familiar, executing my orders without bringing harm to me or my loved ones. In return I would be a kind master and promise, if he remained obedient and faithful, to exalt his seal and his name and redeem his spirit even as my spirit is redeemed.

All being ready in the bedroom *Temple,* I prepared myself to evoke Orobas.

It had been unseasonably warm all day and by late afternoon (when I was ready to operate) the Temple was very hot. After a long ceremonial bath I put on my robe with the obligatory *"By the figurative mystery of this holy vestment..."* and took my position in the circle.

I removed the stopper from the vial of Oil of Abramelin (by tradition the most powerful of Holy Oils, made from 8 parts cinnamon oil, 4 parts myrrh oil, 2 parts oil of galangal, 7 parts olive oil). I anointed the top of my head, then my forehead, throat, heart, solar plexus, navel and groin areas. Wherever it touched my skin, the oil burned like fire and made me excitedly conscious of my psychic centers.

With my Almond Wand I performed the Lesser Banishing Ritual of the Pentagram then proceeded with the *Preliminary Invocation of the Goetia.* This completed, I began to concentrate upon the seal in the Triangle and "call" Orobas.

I don't know what I expected. Nothing was happening. I called Orobas again, this time more forcefully. Still nothing. Disappointment began to settle upon me and I started to feel all the frustration that had brought me to this point. I became impatient and angry. I pointed my Wand toward the Triangle and shouted, "get in the Triangle God damn it or I'll burn your little-ass seal to a crisp. If you aren't for me you're against me and I would just as soon annihilate you than argue with you."

For the first time in my life I had "someone" to vent all my anger and frustration upon. It felt good. It felt *very* good to yell at and threaten someone or some*thing* I held responsible for all my ills.

I don't know how long I raved at that empty cardboard Triangle but suddenly I felt silly. I stopped and took a deep breath. I felt my heart pounding in my throat and I was covered with sweat. In the hot, heavy calm *something* was happening. I didn't see anything but something definitely was in the room with me. It was like the feeling you get when you are awakened from a nap sensing you are not alone, only to discover that your dog is staring at you.

It was in the Triangle. I didn't see it with my eyes like a cartoon or hologram. I saw it like one "sees" an idea—as if it were projected upon the inside back of my skull: a little horse with large sad eyes staring at me like an abused pack animal. Orobas.

I now felt self-conscious, almost embarrassed. Its presence was as objectively perceptible as if another conscious Being stood before me. A Being with an independent existence and feelings. I sensed also that it unquestionably resented being confined in the Triangle.

So stunned was I that for a moment I forgot everything. I completely lost my attitude of superior indignation. Now I was fearful that I would be unable to control the situation. "As long as I stare at the Triangle with all my concentrated will," I thought, "I will stay in control."

No sooner had this thought crossed my mind than a bead of sweat from my brow ran over the bridge of my nose and into my right eye. I blinked several times, then rubbed both eyes with the fingers of my left hand. Suddenly my eyes began to burn so badly that I couldn't keep them open. I instantly realized what I had done. The sweat from my forehead was saturated with Oil of Abramelin. My fingers were covered in it. I was rubbing concentrated cinnamon oil into my own eyes!

The pain was excruciating and getting worse by the second. I was completely blinded. I panicked. I couldn't go on with the evocation like this nor could I risk further breach of procedure by breaking the Circle. The old rage returned. With my eyes squeezed tightly together I turned toward the Triangle and spat a mindless curse at Orobas. I blamed this all on him and vowed to arrange an eternity of confinement and torment if he didn't remain in the Triangle.

I knew that I had no choice but to blindly find my way to the bathroom and wash my eyes. Then the most extraordinary thing happened. I could see. I could see everything. Even with my eyes on "fire" and pressed closed, I could "see" the entire Temple. I saw the incense burning; I saw the Circle; I could even see myself as if from behind and above; I saw Orobas standing in the Triangle.

I was in so much pain that I wasn't at all impressed with this new "magical vision." I had to do something quickly about my eyes. I pointed my wand at the Spirit and barked "stay!" Orobas immediately reclined and remained motionless and peaceful as if he were the little donkey in a nativity scene.

I left the Circle and ran to the bathroom adjacent to the bedroom. I quickly pulled my robe over my head and got into the shower. It was difficult to open my eyes so I held them open with my fingers and allowed the cold water to spray directly on them. I don't know how long I stood there before I felt some relief but it seemed forever.

As I toweled myself dry and put my robe back on the absurdity of my situation became embarrassingly amusing. The picture of me, a grown man, blindly stumbling out of a "Magic Circle" hurling hysterical curses at a demon (that in all probability was just an idea held in a Triangle by my imagination), suddenly became too funny for words.

I looked into the bathroom mirror at my bright red blood-shot eyes and wet hair hanging over my ears and started to laugh hysterically. Some magician.

I felt better now—relieved—as if I experienced a discharge of energy that had been knotted up inside me all my life. Now I couldn't wait to finish the operation.

Back in the Circle all the nervousness that I felt earlier was gone. With cold-blooded resolve I picked up my Wand and addressed Orobas once again. This time there was a clear two-way communication. I mentally spoke my words and "heard" Orobas' response simultaneously:

"I called you forth in good faith. Why did you burn my eyes?"

"You burned your own eyes. Only an idiot would put cinnamon oil on his forehead in this heat."

"If you ever do anything like that again I will destroy you."

"Then I apologize for that which I did not do. Why am I here?"

"Is everything the book tells me about you true?"

"It is…and more."

"Then I tell you, my life is crap. I need to get control of it. I need the 'dignity' to be able to properly care for my family. I need action now. I charge you to muster all the spirits under your control to immediately set to work to correct my situation. I want to see some positive sign *today* that you are working for me."

"But today is too soon." Orobas said calmly. "It is unfair to ask me to work so fast. Give me at least two weeks to show you a sign."

"He's right." I thought to myself. "I *am* asking too much. Maybe I should give him more time. If I don't see any results today, then I will have to admit that this operation is a failure. How will that make me feel? I'm depressed already. I don't know if I could take one more failure. Failure in life, failure in Magick. Maybe I should give him a month—no—six months—yes—six months—something's bound to happen in six months—then I'll be able to say the operation was a success…"

I stopped myself in mid-sentence. These are not my thoughts, they're *his*! This is the classic negotiation process of the Spirits. This is how the magician could be talked into pacts and other such silliness. If I allowed him to go on he could talk me into anything and make me think it was my own idea! It was so subtle yet so obvious. I had to regain control of the conversation.

"No! No more time. I need to see positive proof you are fulfilling your charge and I need to see it today. If I don't, I swear by these red eyes that I will recast the Circle and Triangle for the purpose of burning your seal and annihilating you. On the other hand, if you fulfill your charge I will exalt you and your name. Your seal will live in metal or stone for a thousand years, and you will be redeemed even as I am redeemed. Is that clear?"

"It is clear."

I sent him off with an ad lib *license to depart* and when I could no longer sense his presence I banished the Temple and disassembled the Circle and Triangle.

The entire procedure took a little over an hour. My wife and son were amusing themselves in the living room and were completely unaware of the adventure I had just experienced on the other side of the door.

"What happened to your eyes?" was the only question I was forced to deal with and the entire event almost immediately took on the dimensions of a distant memory.

I got a drink of water and stretched out on the floor to digest what had just happened when we were all startled by the rumblings of what was obviously an old car with a very bad muffler. It coughed and choked to a stop directly in front of our apartment and the driver got out and pounded loudly on our door.

It was "Mad Bob," one of our oldest and dearest friends. He had been out of the country for several years so we were surprised and delighted to see him again. After surviving his lusty bear-hugs we asked him to come in but he said he couldn't stay. He reached into his pocket and took out the keys to his jalopy and tossed them on the couch.

"The car is yours! I'm going to Guatemala. I need to be in Long Beach in a half an hour, give me a ride."

If this wasn't the sign I asked Orobas for it was damned good facsimile. We got into my "new" car and drove to Long Beach where I dropped Mad Bob off to begin his Guatemala adventure. My adventure was just beginning as well.

On the way home, I converted the pennies in the ashtray to a quarter and bought a local newspaper. At home I combed the "Help Wanted" columns and circled three entry-level positions at companies I could now reach in my car. The following day I applied in person at all three and was hired by the third. Three months and three promotions later, I found myself in the engineering department of a large medical device laboratory making a "dignified" wage. During that same period, because of a chain of extraordinary events, I was consecrated Bishop of *Ecclesia Gnostica Catholica.* This "Prelacy" was entirely unexpected and has become one of the most important aspects of my adult life.

Soon after getting my job, I cast the Circle and Triangle and called Orobas again. This time to thank him and tell him I recognized his faithful execution of my charge. I engraved his sigil beautifully upon an attractive tin plate that, barring a direct nuclear hit or a supernova of the Sun, will last a thousand years.

I have called up many of the 72 Spirits over the ensuing years but I have troubled Orobas only a handful of times since (only in times of absolute desperation and after I have exhausted all other means of helping myself). He remains a loyal familiar and has never yet failed in his ability to fulfill his instructions.

The reader can invoke coincidence and argue that all the events subsequent to my evocation were in the process of happening to me anyway. And to this I will not argue. But as much as my left brain interprets such phenomena subjectively—in the terms of psychology, my right brain will always be convinced that there is an objective and independent reality to the Spirits.

As a matter of fact, some of the most competent and experienced Goetic magicians today dismiss the purely psychological explanation as naive. They point out examples of evocations characterized by objects being moved or thrown across the room, power surges, or electric or electronic devices activated or deactivated, and even instances of the Spirit (operating on the magician's instructions) "appearing" before third parties who are unaware of the operation.

Regardless of which theory you embrace, the fact remains that individuals continue to experience perceptible changes in their lives that are identical to the changes they wish to affect by Goetic evocation.

I confess that not every evocation I have performed has been as successful as the Orobas working. On several occasions the "disobedient Spirit" necessitated several conjurations (complete with threats, curses and sigil torture) before the desired result was achieved. Some evocations, I have to admit, have been dismal failures. But even they have yielded much important information. As a matter of fact, I have learned more from the disasters than the triumphs because by reviewing my notes of these events I have been able to draw a profile of what is necessary for success:

1. **Justification.** Is this evocation necessary? Do I deserve the desired object of the operation? Have I done everything I can on the material plane to achieve this result? Or am I lying to myself about my motives and needs?

You must be completely convinced that your demands are absolutely justified. (And don't think we are invoking the great demon "morality" here. An *unnecessary* motive is an *unworthy* motive—pure and simple) When you are truly justified in your demands then you have the momentum of the entire universe behind you.

2. **Emotion.** Unless there is an emotional link to the desired result of the operation, the magician is not tapping that strata of himself (or the spiritual world) where the Spirits of the Goetia reside. The first time you really see a Goetic Spirit you will

feel like you have pulled it out of your *gut* and thrown it in the Triangle.

This is why evocations for the sake of experiment or entertainment seldom achieve satisfactory results and operations of desperation or profound personal need often do.

3. **Will.** It is not enough to be emotionally charged concerning the object of the operation if you are not prepared to do anything about it. The ceremony of evocation must be the unambiguous expression of your absolute Will to effect this change and your willingness to plumb the depths of Hell to see that it is done.

4. **Courage.** "Fear is failure and the forerunner of failure." and Goetic evocations can be very frightening indeed. But if you are *justified* in your need; if it means so much to you that you are charging the ceremony with pure, raw *emotion*; if all this is truly your *Will*—then courage will become your impregnable Circle.

By the same token cowardice will be your undoing. If it is truly your Will to injure your enemy, why go to the trouble to perform a Goetic Evocation when it would be much more effective "magick" to simply confront the person and punch them in the nose. If you think you are going to escape the consequences of this act by sending a Goetic Spirit to do it for you may be unpleasantly surprised.

A WARNING

We have also observed, it is sad to say, that the efficacy of the Art does not always manifest in a positive way in every practitioner's life. Often, either because of inherent character flaws or pre-existing pathologies, the "Spirits" end up running the magician instead of the other way around. It is easy to see that of all branches of ceremonial magick Goetic evocation is among the most likely to be abused, misused and misunderstood.

In retrospect I now see why my teacher was so reluctant to encourage me as a young student to experiment with the Goetia. In her long career she had seen more Goetic disasters than successes and had chosen, probably wisely, to avoid the system altogether.

Often immature dabblers, realizing how easy and effective evocation can be, forego all other aspects of magick including the all important quest for the Knowledge and Conversation of the Holy Guardian Angel. They make Goetia the centerpiece of their magical lives and gather together impressionable, weak-willed individuals to form a "lodge." Impressed by phenomenon that the "master" can easily produce, these individuals often become more his victims than his students. Gone unchecked these relationships eventually become that of master and slave. Unfortunately sincere students often base their entire opinion of ceremonial magick by the pathetic and sophomoric shenanigans of such groups.

The Operator-Receiver technique (usually done with a Magick Mirror in the Triangle) is a very effective and historically valid method of evocation. We feel, however, that the reader is well advised not to seek *preliminary* Goetic instruction from a group or from individuals who offer to "operate" an evocation while you "receive" the vision. Although this technique is very effective, unless you have absolute confidence in the motives and *mental health* of your "operator" you are better off working alone or with a trusted and willing partner of your choice.

The exercises of sexual evocation included later in the book are to be done by two individuals who know and trust each other intimately. Individuals who use Sex Magick, Goetic evocation or indeed, any "magical" lures as "pick up" techniques are all but shouting to the world they are unable to get a sex partner any other way. These are the *last* people on earth from whom anyone should want to be taught Magick.

CHAPTER FIVE

History

If the eye could see the demons that people the universe, existence would be impossible.

— *Talmud,* Berakot, 6

The format of Goetic evocation contains perhaps the most colorful and recognizable elements of any type of Western ceremonial magick. The magician, robed and armed stands inside the Magick Circle protected from the malice of the Spirits by the innumerable Holy Names scrawled thereupon. Several feet away stands the Spirit trapped inside the Triangle of the Art. With his Wand upraised the magician issues his commands and the Spirit reluctantly obeys. This is the stuff of "Sword and Sorcerer" movies. Yet this is precisely the method, and it has come down to us in a most extraordinary way.

Sixteenth and seventeenth Century Europe abounded with a myriad of practitioners of the magical arts who, for the most part, were inspired by the colorful images of Middle-Eastern magic.

We must keep in mind that for many years much of Iberian Peninsula was occupied by the Moslems. Ironically, even though Islamic law dictates strict proscriptions against unorthodox spiritual practices, the occupation forces tolerated a handful of Spanish communities where a certain level of spiritual freedom flourished.

These pockets of liberality attracted not only the innovative practitioners of the "Black Arts," but also the Jewish Qabalists whose wisdom was, for the first time, committed to writing. This period was to profoundly influence the Renaissance and subsequently the entire "Hermetic" traditions of Western Civilization.

It is from this tradition that the concept of "Solomonic" magic was developed. Spirits (genies) trapped in bottles, magic carpets, great treasures protected by demons—all reminiscent of *A Thousand and One Arabian Nights*.

The text that has become known as the *Goetia* is the first book of what is commonly referred to as the *Lemegeton*, a collection of five texts traditionally attributed to King Solomon. The most popular versions (including the one Crowley hired S.L. MacGregor Mathers to translate) are drawn primarily from translations of Sloane Manuscripts nos. 2731 and 3648 in the possession of the British Library.

Few individuals today are so naive as to believe that the author was indeed the legendary Hebrew King. Indeed, there is no evidence to demonstrate that the five texts are even the work of a single author or that the authors were even practicing magicians. In fact, by the very nature of the translations it is obvious that the scribe or scribes were decidedly hostile toward the art. Many of the Spirits are clearly the Gods and Goddesses of older religions who were "banished" to the infernal regions by the new Order. Many of the Dukes especially seem to have been originally female in character (a most dangerous spiritual idea to lonely monastic scribes prone to fantasies).

Magic books attributed to King Solomon circulated through-out Europe since at least the middle of the Sixteenth Century. Sloane 2731 dates from 1687 and most likely is the result of one practitioner's desire to have his favorite "Solomonic" works bound conveniently into one volume.

It also appears that he used the opportunity to update the texts by revising the language and using the vernacular of the day. As archaic as the language appears to us today, The

Lemegeton represents a "new, improved" Seventeenth Century version of far older material. How old, we cannot say.[8]

The Magical Revival of the late 1800s resulted in new translations and the *Lemegeton* and the *Goetia* emerged from near complete obscurity and into the light of *relative* obscurity and students and practitioners of the occult have been tantalized by its mysteries ever since.

Modern editions of the *Goetia* remain in print and continue to sell very well (almost every student of magick worth his/her salt owns at least one copy), yet relatively few individuals actually have participated in a Goetic evocation. The reasons are many but perhaps the single most compelling excuse is rooted in the mistaken belief that in order to succeed in evocation one must conform exactly with the procedures and conjurations outlined in the text.

The seemingly endless pages of tedious, archaic and parochial conjurations, constraints, exorcisms and curses continue to bewilder and discourage 99% of would-be Goetic magicians. *And that is precisely what they are meant to do!*

THEORY

The Universe was very simple from the traditional Goetic magician's point of view. Above him was God, the creator of the world and the ultimate source of his authority. Below the magician was an "infernal" world, inhabited by demon spirits who were once "Angels of the Lord" but now exiled from heaven as punishment for their pride and disobedience. Their "fall" established the inter-dependent threefold "world" in which we find ourselves; Heaven, Earth, and Hell.

---

[8] For the convenience of the modern reader we have also put the translated material in Chapter Eight in modern vernacular and, where obvious, returned certain Spirits to their original gender.

Like the Titans of Greek Mythology, the Infernal Spirits (not God) are responsible for the maintenance of the material world including the "earthly-fleshly" nature of Man.

As a resident of the Earth, the magician stands between the Divine and the Infernal Worlds. If he is pious before the eyes of his "God" then he has the Divine authority to order and control the lower spirits.

To achieve this authoritative state of mind the magicians of old recited lengthy litanies of affirmations and self-aggrandizements, itemizing their high morals and examples of their religious piety. ("You obeyed Moses, you obeyed Aaron, you'll obey me too!")

Once he had convinced *himself* that he had the authority to command the Spirit, the magician next had to achieve the subjective state of mind whereby he could actually "see" it. This he induced by the use of "magic words" which he recited much like a mantra. In this way, he created a strange and mystic atmosphere in which nothing was impossible and anything could happen.

Standing in the Circle, protected by the Divine names with which he had aligned himself, the magician (pumped up by affirmations and "intoxicated" by the magic words) concentrated upon the Triangle until the Spirit appeared. The universally holy virtues of all things triune was enough to trap the Spirit in the Triangle long enough to receive the Charge from the magician. After receiving his orders the Spirit was given License to Depart to go forth and do the magician's bidding.

The text of the *Goetia* is filled with the details of such operations—page after page of formal Conjurations, Constraints, Invocations, Curses, Greater Curses, Addresses to the Spirit on his arrival and departure, etc.

PRACTICE

There exist today, Goetic magicians (both solitary practitioners and organized groups) who operate strictly "by the book."

The Circle, the Triangle and all the diagrams are constructed exactly as illustrated in the *Goetia*. They recite (or most often read) the conjurations, constraints and curses exactly as written in the 1687 text. Ceremonies of some of these magicians are a thrill to behold and, without a doubt, the Art will forever be perpetuated in its classic form because of their dedicated labor.

It must be pointed out, however, that there is absolutely no necessity (nor particular advantage) to blindly conforming with the Conjuration scripts of the ancient texts. The Spirits are no more impressed if you say "thee" and "thine" than they are if you say "you" and "yours."

Aleister Crowley was aware of this and crafted several versions of his own conjurations. In fact, as we shall see later, in his own copy of the *Goetia* he simply hand copied the Second Key of the Enochian system. It is our opinion (and that of other Crowley scholars) that for personal Goetic conjurations Crowley most likely in his later years discarded the traditional conjurations and simply recited the First and Second Enochian Calls.

It is also our opinion that the most effective conjurations are of the magician's own design. We encourage the reader, once the fundamentals of the system are thoroughly grasped, to create your own conjuration which, like your Temple, equipment, and procedures, is uniquely yours.

CHAPTER SIX

Minimum Requirements

Even though we believe that the Conjurations and certain other components of the Sloane material are anachronistically superfluous to modern Goetic evocation, we are not suggesting that the basic elements of the system are not sound. On the contrary, the fundamentals of the classic procedure are extremely important. We do feel it is very important to encourage the reader to break free from the superstitious idea that magick will only work by blind conformity to any dictated procedure (new or old). The understanding of what is truly necessary and what is not is what separates the real magician from a character in a role-playing game.

THE TEMPLE

The Temple need only be a room large enough to accommodate the Circle and Triangle. A living room, a bedroom or a similar area where privacy can be achieved is sufficient. If there is other furniture in the room care must be taken to clear the room of clutter and any appearance of disorder. (Often a room is more efficiently banished by a good dusting and vacuuming than by the banishing ritual itself.)

THE CIRCLE

In a very real sense the Circle is not the chalk or tape on the floor but the aura of the magician himself. It not only defines and circumscribes all that he or she is, it stands as a fortress against all that is "outside."

The Circle is the magician's universe and the center of the Circle is the point of supreme balance, the fulcrum from which he moves the worlds. For the purpose of Goetic evocation the Circle is *not optional*. It is a fundamental requirement in the Temple for it is the safety zone in which the magician can stand with complete confidence to command the forces trapped in the Triangle.

Upon the floor of your Temple draw, tape, paint, scratch or otherwise create a Circle approximately nine feet in diameter. Approximately six inches inside the circumference draw another Circle. In the space between the circles place the Holy Names of your choice.

It would be presumptuous for us to suggest to the reader what Holy Names are most appropriate. It is each magician's quest to determine for him/herself which "Deity or Deities" are harmonious with the magician's own magical universe. The Circle itself is a perfect symbol of divinity. A simple unbroken line with no names at all can be sufficient for individuals whose realization of this abstraction is profound. I have used on occasion a thin silk cord which, after the ceremony (when I felt it advantageous to stay in the Circle for hours or days), I have wrapped around myself as a belt.

The classic Circle was that of a coiled serpent upon whose body was written—in Hebrew—the Deity, Angel, and Arch-angel Names attributed to the first nine Sephiroth of the Tree of Life. The space between the circles was bright, deep yellow. The lettering was in black. The classic Circle also enclosed four Hexagrams positioned at the quarters and was surrounded by four Pentagrams positioned at the cross-quarters.

Examples of traditional and modern magical Circles can be found in the Appendix.

THE TRIANGLE

Like the Circle, the Triangle is *not optional*. It is the area in which the Spirit appears and is compelled to obedience. (See the Appendix.)

In the East (or in the indicated direction of the particular Spirit in question) about two feet from the Circle, draw, tape, paint, scratch or otherwise create a Triangle, each side measuring three feet. The Triangle's base shall be toward the Circle. Upon each side of the Triangle place the Three Holy Names of your choice.

The classic Goetic Triangle was surrounded by three names: **ANAPHAXETON** (Great God of all the Heavenly Host) to the left, **PRIMEUMATON** (the First and the Last) at the base, and **TETRAGRAMMATON** (the ineffable God name Y.H.V.H.) to the right. Inside the classic Triangle, at the points, were placed the letters **MI–CHA–EL** (the Archangel Michael). In the center was a circle. The circle in the center of the Triangle was green (the remainder of the inside was white) and the names on the outside of were written in red.

As mentioned earlier, the names around the Circle are entirely the prerogative of each magician. You might ask yourself what qualities, virtues, or powers you hold sacred in your own magical disciplines: LOVE–WILL–UNION; FAITH–HOPE–CHARITY; SAT–CHIT–ANANDA; or words, numbers or formulae which represent such things, could work nicely if they are meaningful to you. The almost infinite metaphysical virtues of a triangle make it a perfect device to confine and control that which has never been confined and controlled by you. For many magicians a simple Triangle with a circle in the center suffices quite nicely (with or without the surrounding names).

Incense may also be placed inside the Triangle but once the Temple is opened and the Spirit conjured the magician *should not leave* the Circle or reach into the Triangle.

THE SEAL OF THE SPIRIT

Upon the circle of the Triangle will rest the Seal or Sigil of the Spirit drawn upon parchment. These symbols are derived from the traditional *Lemegeton* material and theoretically are the living representations of the Spirits. Some texts dictate that it be made of virgin calf-skin parchment and the drawing done with the blood of an owl or some other beast. Such heroics we feel were intended as "fool traps" and are unnecessary for modern workings. But if you would feel better about the operation if you used the virgin calf-skin, please go ahead.

After the ceremony you should take pains to house the Seal in a special container. You should never be careless with an "activated" Seal or forget where you put it. Depending upon the purpose of the evocation you may wish to carry the Seal upon your person or attach it to an object relating to the operation.

I have learned from bitter experience that it is unwise to have *two operators* in a single operation or to give or loan an activated Seal to another person. It is hard enough to keep your own Will directed toward the one purpose of the operation. I have found it impossible for two individuals to be so unified in their magical resolve as to gain joint control over a Goetic Spirit. (This does not apply to an operation utilizing an operator and a receiver or to sexual Goetia workings such as are described later in this book.)

THE HEXAGRAM OF SOLOMON

The Golden Dawn defined the Hexagram as "...a powerful symbol representing the operation of the Seven Planets under the presidency of the Sephiroth..." This very recognizable symbol of Judaism, sometimes called the Shield of David, is a most appropriate emblem of the Divine Macrocosm (The big world of God, represented in ancient times by the Sun surrounded by the six then-known Planets. (see Appendix).

The Goetic magician wears the Hexagram on the skirt of his or her robe to act as a shield or badge of authority. By displaying the Hexagram to the Spirit the magician proves he or she is part of and representative of the Macrocosmic Order with full power to exercise that authority. Upon seeing the Hexagram the Spirits (by tradition) are compelled to take on human form.

The classic Hexagram was painted upon calfskin parchment and was covered with linen.

Modern magicians should feel free to make the Hexagram as ornate or as simple as they see fit but by *no means should omit* this very important magical device.

THE PENTAGRAM OF SOLOMON

The Golden Dawn defined the Pentagram as "...a powerful symbol representing the operation of the Eternal Spirit and the Four Elements under the Presidency of the letters of the Name Yeheshuah..." (see Appendix).

In contrast to the Hexagram, the Pentagram is the symbol of the Microcosm (the little world of Man) represented by the four elements of Fire, Water, Air and Earth governed by the Fifth element of Spirit.

As Hexagram affirms that the magician is in harmony with the Macrocosmic Order, the Pentagram affirms that he is Master of the Microcosmic Order. By wearing these two symbols the magician is reminded that he or she is positioned between Heaven and Hell, Executor of the Gods and Master of the Demons.

The Goetia says that the Pentagram should be engraved upon a medallion of silver or gold and worn around the neck. On the flip side of the medallion should be engraved the Seal of the Spirit being evoked.

Many modern magicians prefer to construct the medallion from the Spirit's appropriate metal (gold for Kings, copper for Dukes, etc.). The Pentagram engraved upon the front side, the Spirit's Seal on the back.

OTHER REQUIREMENTS

THE WAND

The Greater Key of Solomon describes the Wand and many other magical weapons in great detail. It is accurate to say that to follow the instructions for their construction to the letter would require many months (if not years) to accomplish. It is generally agreed that such instructions are red herrings designed to discourage the dull and unworthy.

The Wand is the weapon of the magician's will and is the instrument with which he conjures. (The Sword, while effective for banishing and intimidation, is not the weapon for Conjuration.) Usually the Wand is approximately the length of the magician's arm measured from the finger tips to the elbow. Traditionally it is made of a straight branch of Almond or Hazel wood and is approximately the diameter of the magician's little finger.

THE MAGIC RING OR DISC

There are Goetic magicians who say the Magic Ring is an unnecessary addition to the list of magical weapons. And, personally, I have never encountered any Spirit from whom I have needed to protect myself against their "stinking sulphurous fumes and flaming breath." Nevertheless I have always had the Ring at hand when evoking any of the Spirits for whom the text says the Ring is required. (see Appendix).

One of the most adept Goetic magicians I have ever met related a remarkable tale of his experience with the Magic Ring.

While evoking Astaroth[9], he became so enamored by the Spirit's beauty that he forgot the purpose of the evocation. He said that the Temple was filled with an intoxicating perfume

---

[9] No matter what the text may say, Astaroth is the thinly disguised version of the Goddess Astarte, who is anything but a frightening monster.

which seem to issue from her lovely mouth and that as she spoke to him his only thought was that he had to somehow make physical love to her.

It was only by accident that his eyes fell upon the Magic Ring and he recognized the need for him to hold it up before his face—not to protect himself from the stinking breath of a monster but to help himself "snap out of it" before he was lured from the Circle to try to make love to the Spirit in the Triangle.

The above experience and that of others indicate that the Magic Ring should be included in the Goetic magician's arsenal of weapons.

The original text says it is made of gold or silver (of course) and was bright yellow with black lettering. But we feel that any material, even paper, will be effective.

THE BRASS BOTTLE

According to tradition Solomon sealed up the Evil Spirits in a "Vessel of Brass" and sealed it with a leaden seal. While the occasion seldom arises for its use, a small brass bottle can be employed if necessary against disobedient Spirits as a threat or a punishment device. The Seal of the Spirit is placed inside the bottle and a lead cap placed upon the top. In cases of extreme disobedience the lead cap can be melted into place. [Once, to threaten a particularly hostile Spirit, I placed his Seal in the bottle; rested the lead cap on the mouth of the bottle; placed the bottle on an unlighted piece of self igniting charcoal; placed the charcoal upon a bed of match heads in the censer; and placed the censer in the Triangle with pieces of stick incense burning perpetually just inches over this whole assembly. The idea being that if even one burning incense stick were to drop an ash still containing a little coal, it would ignite the match heads, igniting the charcoal, heating up the brass bottle, eventually melting the lead seal into place. I (and my remarkably understanding wife) kept the incense sticks burning for three days before the task I had charged the Spirit with was finally executed.]

THE ROBE

The classic outfit includes a long linen robe (white), a cap or a mitre and belt made from a lion's skin upon which are written all the names which are upon the Circle.

Any robe that holds for you magical significance is appropriate for Goetic evocation. A simple white robe is excellent. If you belong to a magical society or hold personal degrees, the robe and insignia of your Grade is most appropriate.

If you look good, you will feel good. It is not a good idea to overdress to the degree that you feel silly or pretentious.

CHAPTER SEVEN

The Preliminary Invocation
of the Goetia

𝕬 s we indicated in Chapter Four, the first requisite for a successful Goetic evocation is to firmly establish your power and declare your authority to command the Spirits. Below is an annotated version of *The Preliminary Invocation of the Goetia*,[10] a version of the Bornless Ritual of the Golden Dawn, modified by Aleister Crowley for use as a preliminary ritual for not only Goetic workings, but for more exalted operations including the invocation of one's Holy Guardian Angel. (See Crowley's *Liber Samech*.)

It is easy to see that this ceremony serves as both Temple Opening and Declaration of Authority. Also the Barbarous Names of Evocation serve to "intoxicate" the mind of the magician and evoke the necessary state of consciousness.

Done correctly, (after the Banishing Ritual of the Pentagram) we believe it is the only ceremony necessary prior to calling the particular Spirit. It has been our experience that once the Preliminary Invocation of the Goetia has been recited one need only call the Spirit by name to succeed in evoking it into the Triangle. Repetition of the **"Hear me..."** rubric is generally enough to compel the most reluctant Spirits to obedience.

The Invocation was modified by Crowley to conform with the Deities and formulas of Thelema and the New Aeon. If you

---

[10] From a Fragment of a *Graeco-Egyptian Work upon Magic*, originally translated by C.W. Goodwin, 1852. Crowley would later adapt it as the core text of *Liber Samech*.

are not a Thelemite and have another religion or spiritual discipline by which you are empowered, this ceremony is easily modified to accommodate your deities and formula.

Begin at the center of the circle in the square of Tiphareth. Recite what is in **bold type** only. All of the necessary elements of this ritual which are not in text can be found in the Appendix.

THE PRELIMINARY INVOCATION OF THE GOETIA (NOTES FROM LIBER SAMECH)

by Aleister Crowley

HEKAS HEKAS ESTI BEBILOI

THE OATH

Thee I invoke, the Bornless One.
Thee, that didst create the Earth and Heavens.
Thee, that didst create the Night and the Day.
Thee, that didst create the Darkness and the Light.
Thou art RA-HOOR-KHUIT, Myself made perfect,
      whom no man hath seen at any time.
Thou art IA-BESZ, the Truth in Matter
Thou art IA-APOPHRASZ, the Truth in Motion
Thou hast distinguished between the Just and the Unjust
Thou didst make the Female and the Male.
Thou didst produce the Seeds and the Fruit
Thou didst form Men to love one another, and to hate
      one another.

I am (motto) **thy Prophet, unto whom Thou didst commit Thy Mysteries, the Ceremonies of Khem.** (Thelema or your particular magical discipline.)

Hear Thou Me, for I am the Angle of Nu, Angel of Had, Angel of Ra-Hoor-Khu: (or the divine names of your tradition) **These are Thy True Names, handed down to the Prophets of Khem** (or as above).

(Pass widdershins [counter-clockwise] to East.)

—𝕬IR—

(Make equilibrating Pentagram of
Spirit Active; see Appendix.)

EHEIEH

(Make the Sign of the Rending of the Veil; see Appendix.)

(Make invoking Pentagram of Air, see Appendix.)

IHVH

(Give sign of Shu; see Appendix.)

Hear Me:
AR ThIAO RHEIBET A-ThELE-BER-SET A BELAThA ABEU EBEU PhI-ThETA-SOE IB ThIAO

Hear me, and make all Spirits subject unto Me; so that every Spirit of the Firmament and of the Ether; upon the Earth and under the Earth, on dry land and in the Water; of Whirling Air, and of rushing Fire, and every Spell and Scourge of God may be obedient unto Me.

(Pass widdershins to South.)

—𝕱IRE—

(Make equilibrating Pentagram of Spirit Active.)

EHEIEH

(Make the Sign of the Rending of the Veil.)

(Make invoking Pentagram of Fire.)

ELOHIM

(Give sign of Thoum-aesh-neith.)

I invoke Thee, the Terrible and Invisible God: who dwellest in the Void Place of the Spirit:

AR-O-GO-GO-RU-ABRAO SOTOU MUDORIO PhALARThAO OOO AEPE

The Bornless One.

Hear me, and make all Spirits subject unto Me; so that every Spirit of the Firmament and of the Ether; upon the Earth and under the Earth, on dry land and in the Water; of Whirling Air, and of rushing Fire, and every Spell and Scourge of God may be obedient unto Me.

(Pass widdershins to the West.)

—𝔚ATER—

(Make equilibrating Pentagram of Spirit, Passive.)

AGLA

(Make the Sign of the Closing of the Veil.)

(Make invoking Pentagram of Water.)

EL

(Give sign Auramot.)

Hear Me:
RU-ABRA-IAO MRIODOM BABALON-BAL-BIN-ABAOT. ASAL-ON-AI APhEN-IAO I PhOTETh ABRASAX AEOOU ISChURE

Mighty and Bornless One!

Hear me, and make all Spirits subject unto Me; so that every Spirit of the Firmament and of the Ether; upon the Earth and under the Earth, on dry land and in the Water; of Whirling Air, and of rushing Fire, and every Spell and Scourge of God may be obedient unto Me.

(Pass widdershins to the North.)

— ℭARTH —

(Make equilibrating Pentagram of Spirit, Passive.)

AGLA

(Make the Sign of the Closing of the Veil.)

(Make invoking Pentagram of Earth.)

ADONAI

(Give sign of Set.)

I Invoke Thee:
MA BARRAIO IOEL KOThA AThOR-E-BAL-O-ABRAOT.

Hear me, and make all Spirits subject unto Me; so that every Spirit of the Firmament and of the Ether; upon the Earth and under the Earth, on dry land and in the Water; of Whirling Air, and of rushing Fire, and every Spell and Scourge of God may be obedient unto Me.

(Pass widdershins and return to Square of Tiphareth.)

(Make equilibrating Pentagram of Spirit Active.)

EHEIEH

(Make the Sign of the Rending of the Veil.)

(Make Sign of the Sun and Moon Conjoined.)

(Give Signs of LVX.)

Hear Me:
AOT ABAOT BAS-AUMGN. ISAK SA-BA-OT.

(Fall prostrate in adoration.)

This is the Lord of the Gods
This is the Lord of the Universe
This is He whom the Winds fear. This is He, who having made voice by His commandment is the Lord of all Things: King, Ruler and Helper.

Hear me, and make all Spirits subject unto Me; so that every Spirit of the Firmament and of the Ether; upon the Earth and under the Earth, on dry land and in the Water; of Whirling Air, and of rushing Fire, and every Spell and Scourge of God may be obedient unto me.

—SPIRIT—

(Make equilibrating Pentagram of Spirit, Passive.)

AGLA

(Make the Sign of the Closing of the Veil.)

(Make Sign of the Sun and Moon Conjoined.)

(Give Signs of LVX.)

Hear Me:
IEOU PUR IOU PUR IAOTh IAEO IOOU ABRASAX SABRIAM OO UU AD-ON-A-I EDE EDU ANGELOS TON ThEON ANLALA LAI GAIA AEPE DIATHARNA THORON.

(Resume Standing.)

I am He! the Bornless Spirit! having sight in the feet: strong, and the Immortal Fire!

I am He! the Truth!

I am He! who hate that evil should be wrought in the World!

I am He, that lighteneth and thundereth!

I am He, From whom is the Shower of the Life of Earth!

I am He, whose mouth ever flameth!

I am He, the Begetter and Manifester unto the Light!

I am He, The Grace of the Worlds!

"The Heart Girt with a Serpent" is my name!

Come thou forth, and follow me: and make all Spirits Subject unto Me so that every Spirit of the Firmament, and of the Ether, upon the Earth and under the Earth: on dry

Land, or in the Water: of Whirling Air or of Rushing Fire, and every Spell and Scourge of God may be obedient unto me!

IAO: SABAO
Such are the Words!

THE CONJURATION

After the Preliminary Invocation of the Goetia the magician should be in a powerfully exalted state of mind. One now should know beyond the shadow of a doubt that he or she has the spiritual authority to command the Spirits and that no Spirit will be able to resist the Conjuration. It is enough at this point to point your Wand toward the Triangle and say something like:

Hear me, O Spirit (Name), and appear before this Circle in a fair human form. Come peaceably and visibly, before me in the Triangle of art.

Repeat the Spirit's name several times until you "see" or sense the Spirit in the Triangle.

It should be noted that a large portion of the original Goetia is dedicated to stronger and stronger Conjurations and Curses intended to be used if the Spirit is reluctant to come. If it still does not appear there are even invocations of the King who is the "boss" of your Spirit.

The mere existence of these extra Conjurations is enough to create a level of doubt in the mind of the magician that his first Conjuration might not be strong enough. If you are worried from the start that your Conjuration will not work, *then chances are it won't.*

We strongly suggest that you keep your Conjuration short and simple and that you recite it immediately after the Preliminary Invocation when your strength is at its peak.

If it is obvious that the Spirit has not obeyed your Conjuration; if you are *sure* that there is not something (visible or invisible) in the Triangle you may simply declare that since the Spirit will not co-operate with you, then you have no choice but to annihilate it and remove it forever from your universe.

"If you are not for me, you are against me and if you do not immediately comply with my wishes I will burn your Seal to ashes and remove you forever from my Universe."

It has been our experience that this simple threat is enough to make the most uncooperative Spirit "appear." Usually at this point the Spirit wants to appear, get it's orders and get out of there. Memorization of the lengthy Conjurations of the classical texts are only necessary if the magician's sense of Art demands it.

Below is a Conjuration adapted by Aleister Crowley and translated by him into the "Angelic" language of Enochian. Crowley obviously felt that the Enochian language had more universal applications than just those relating to Enochian Magick. As a matter of fact, as we mentioned earlier, there is every reason to believe that when Crowley performed Goetic Evocation he simply used the First and Second Call of the Enochian System. (See *The Enochian World of Aleister Crowley: Enochian Sex Magick*, The Original Falcon Press, and following the Conjuration below.)

We have arranged the Conjuration with the English translation appearing directly below each line of Enochian. We have done our best to make the translation clear enough for the reader to customize a conjuration of their own. As you can see, Crowley has occasionally simplified or paraphrased portions of the text. If you would like to learn more about Enochian Magick, we encourage you to refer to the above mentioned text which includes an excellent Enochian dictionary.

The First Conjuration

(Enochian and English)

Ol vinu od zodakame, Ilasa,   Gahé N: od
I invoke and move thee, O thou, Spirit N: and

elanusahé   vaoresagi   Iaida,
being exalted above ye   in the power of   the Most High,

gohusa pujo ilasa, darebesa! do-o-i-apé
I say   unto thee,   Obey!   in the name

Beralanensis, Baldachiensis, Paumachia, od
Beralanesis,   Baldachiensis, Paumachia, and

Apologiae Sedes: od   micaelzodo   aretabasa
Apologiae Sedes: and   of the mighty ones   who govern

gahé, mire Liachidae   od   qouódi   Salamanu
spirits,   Liachidae and ministers of the House

telocahé: od   Tabaäme   Otahila   Apologiae
of Death: and   by the Chief Prince of the seat of Apologia

do em Poamala,   ol vinu-ta   od   zodaméta!
in the Ninth Legion, I invoke thee and   conjure thee!

Od   elanusahé   vaoresagi   Iaida,
And   being exalted above ye   in the power of the Most High,

gohusa pujo ilasa, darebesa! do-o-i-apé   totza   das
I say   unto thee,   Obey!   in the name   of him   who

cameliatza od   asá,   kasaremé tofagilo   od   tolergi
spake   and it was, to whom all creatures and   things

darebesa. Pilahé ol, das Iada   oela   azodiazodore
obey.   Moreover I, whom God   made   in the likeness of

Iada, das i qo-o-al   marebi   totza   jijipahé,
God,   who is the creator according to his   living breath,

larinuji ilasa   do-o-i-apé das   i   salada
stir thee up   in the name which is   the voice of wonder

micaelazodo   Iada, El, micaelzodo od   adapehaeta:
of the mighty God, El,   strong   and unspeakable:

ilasa   gahé N.   Od ol gohusa   pujo ilasa, darebesa,
O thou Spirit N.   And I   say   unto thee,   obey,

do-o-i-apé totza   das cameliatza od   isa;   od do
in the name of him who   spake   and it was; and in

vomesareji,   do-o-i-ainu Iada! Phiahé   do-o-i-apé
every one of ye, O ye names of God! Moreover in the names

Adonai,   El, Elohim, Elohi, Ehyeh Asher Ehyeh,
Adonai,   El, Elohim, Elohi, Ehyeh Asher Ehyeh,

Zabaoth, Elion, Iah, Tetragrammaton, Shaddai,
Zabaoth, Elion, Iah, Tetragrammaton,   Shaddai,

Enayo   Iad   Iaida,   ol larinuji ilasa;   od
Lord   God   Most High, I   stir thee up;   and

do-vameoepelifa gohus, darbesa! ilasa   gahé N.
in   our strength I say, Obey!   O thou   Spirit N.

Zodameranu ca-no-quoda   olé   oanio;   asapeta
Appear   unto His servants in   a moment; before

komeselahe azodiazodore   olalore; od
the circle   in the likeness of a man; and

fetahé-are-zodi.   Od   do-o-a-ipé   adapehaheta
visit me in peace. And   in the name ineffable

Tetragrammaton Jehovah, gohus, darbesa! soba
Tetragrammation Iehovah, I say, Obey!   whose

sapahé   elonusahinu   nazoda   poilapé,
mighty sound being exalted in power the pillars are divided,

zodonugonu caelazod   holado; pereje je-ialaponu;
the winds of the firmament groan aloud; fire burns not;

caosaga zodaca   do- jizodajazoda;   od   tofajilo
the earth moves   in   earthquakes;   and   all things

Salamann   perepesol   od   caosaji, od   faorejita
of the house   of heaven   and   earth, and   the dwelling-place

oresa   cahisa ta   jizodajazoda,   od   cahisa   do-mire,
of darkness are as   earthquakes,   and   are   in torment,

od   ovankaho   do-koratzo.   Niisa   eca,   ilasa gahé N.
and are confounded   in thunder. Come therefore, O   spirit N.

olé   oanio: christeos   faorejita   afafa,
in   a moment: let thy   dwelling-place   be empty,

imumamare   Iaida, od   darebesa   na-e-el.
apply unto us the secrets of Truth, and   obey   my power.

Nissa,   fatahe - are - zodi, zodameranu   pujo
Come forth,   visit us   in   peace,   appear   unto

ooaona; zodoreje: darebesa   jijipahé!   Lapé ol
my eyes; be friendly: Obey   the living breath!   For   I

larinuji-ta   do-o-i-apé   Iada Vaoanu   das   apila,
stir thee up in the name of the God of Truth who liveth forever,

Helioren.   Darebesa   jijipahé,   eca,
Helioren.   Obey   the living breath, therefore,

do-miame   pujo   valasa,   ta   anugelareda:
continually   unto   the end,   as   my thoughts:

zodameranu ooanoa: zodoreje: gohola   iaiada
appear   to my eyes: be friendly: speaking secrets of Truth

do-bianu   od   do-omepe!
in voice   and   in understanding!

Below are the First and Second Calls of the Enochian system which also can serve as excellent Goetic Conjurations. As stated earlier the Second Call was copied by Crowley on the inside back cover of his own copy of the Goetia.

Magicians wishing to utilize the Calls as conjurations should insert the following immediately after the Preliminary Invocation of the Goetia.

THE OPENING OF THE PORTAL
OF THE VAULT OF THE ADEPTS
PAROKETH, the Veil of the Sanctuary.
The Sign of the Rending of the Veil.
The Sign of the Closing of the Veil.
[Give these.]
Make the Invoking Pentagrams of Spirit.
In the number 21, in the grand word AHIH;
In the Name YHShVH, in the Pass Word I.N.R.I.,

O Spirits of the Tablet of Spirit,
Ye, ye, I invoke!
The sign of Osiris slain!
The sign of the mourning of Isis!
The sign of Apophis and Typhon!
The sign of Osiris Risen!
L.V.X., Lux. The Light of the Cross.
[Give these.]

In the name of IHVH ALVH VDOTh, I declare that the Spirits
of Spirit have been duly invoked. The Knock
1—4444.

ℭHE 𝔍IRST 𝔎EY

OL sonuf vaoresaji, gohu IAD Balata, elanusaha caelazod:
sobrazod-ol Roray i ta nazodapesad, Giraa ta maelpereji, das
hoel-qo qaa notahoa zodimezod, od comemahe ta nobeloha
zodien; soba tahil ginonupe pereje aladi, das vaurebes obolehe
giresam. Casarem ohorela caba Pire: das zodonurenusagi cab:
erem Iadanahe. Pilahe farezodem zodenurezoda adana gono
Iadapiel das home-tohe: soba ipame lu ipamis: das sobolo vepe
zodomeda poamal, od bogira aai ta piape Piamoel od Vaoan
(or Vooan in invocations of Fallen Spirits)! Zodacare, eca, od
zodameranu! odo cicale Qaa; zodoreje, lape zodiredo Noco
Mada, Hoathahe I A I D A!

THE FIRST KEY
(English)

I REIGN over ye, saith the God of Justice, in power exalted above the Firmament of Wrath, in whose hands the Sun is as a sword, and the Moon as a through thrusting Fire: who measureth your Garments in the midst of my Vestures, and trussed you together as the palms of my hands. Whose seats I garnished with the Fire of Gathering, and beautified your garments with admiration. To whom I made a law to govern the Holy Ones, and delivered ye a Rod, with the Ark of Knowledge. Moreover you lifted up your voices and sware obedience and faith to Him that liveth and triumpheth: whose beginning is not, nor end cannot be: which shineth as a flame in the midst of your palaces, and reigneth amongst you as the balance of righteousness and truth!

Move therefore, and shew yourselves! Open the mysteries of your creation! Be friendly unto me, for I am the Servant of the same your God: the true worshipper of the Highest!

THE SECOND KEY

ADAGITA vau-pa-ahe zodonugonu fa-a-ipe salada! Vi-i-vau el! Sobame ial-pereji i-zoda-zodazod pi-adapehe casarema aberameji ta ta-labo paracaleda qo-ta lores-el-qo turebesa ooge balatohe! Giui cahisa lusada oreri od micalapape cahisa bia ozodonugonu! lape noanu tarofe coresa tage o-quo maninu IA-I-DON. Torezodu! gohe-el, zodacare eca ca-no-quoda! zodameranu micalazodo od ozadazodame vaurelar; lape zodir IOIAD!

THE SECOND KEY
(English)

CAN the Wings of the Winds understand your voices of Wonder? O you! the second of the First! whom the burning

flames have framed in the depth of my Jaws! Whom I have
prepared as cups for a wedding, or as the flowers in their
beauty for the chamber of Righteousness! Stronger are your
feet than the barren stone: and mightier are your voices than
the manifold winds! For you are become a building such as is
not, save in the Mind of the All-Powerful.

Arise, saith the First: Move therefore unto his servants! Shew
yourselves in power, and make me a strong Seer-of-things: for
I am of Him that liveth for ever!

𝕿HE 𝕮HARGE 𝕿O 𝕿HE 𝕾PIRIT

Therefore fear not the Spirits, but be firm and courteous with them;
for thou hast no right to despise or revile them; and this too may
lead thee astray. Command and banish them, curse them by the
Great Names if need be; but neither mock nor revile them, for so
assuredly wilt thou be the led into error.
— Aleister Crowley, *Liber Librae,*
adapted from a Golden Dawn Document

You may or may not actually "see" the Spirit in the Triangle.
Most often you will first sense the presence in the Triangle and
then an image may begin to appear in the incense smoke. If
you utilize a Black Mirror in the Triangle most often you will
see at least some distortion of your own image but if you
expect to immediately see a solidly projected cartoon or holo-
graphic image in the Triangle you are most likely going to be
disappointed.

We feel it is a mistake to take up too much time and energy
trying to force yourself to *see* the Spirit. You are here to
command a Spirit, not to explore a vision.

When you feel certain that the Spirit is in the Triangle,
welcome it graciously and thank it for coming.

Proceed immediately to issue your instructions. Word your commands in such a way as to avoid ambiguities that will provide loopholes which the Spirit may use to avoid fulfilling the intention of your instructions. (The classic story of the *Monkey's Paw* serves as an excellent example.) Never fail to stipulate that you want your instructions carried out without harm to you or you loved-ones.

Give specific time limitations on when you want your instructions executed. Tell the Spirit in no uncertain terms that if it disobeys the instructions and does not meet the deadline, that you will conjure it again and issue a very strict ultimatum. (If this becomes necessary do not fail to do so exactly when you told it you would. Tell it you are giving it one more opportunity to fulfill it's charge or you will slowly burn it's Seal until it is utterly destroyed. Do not bluff. If you say you are going to do something, do it.)

IMPORTANT: Stay in control of the situation. Every aspect of the evocation must be on the magician's terms. Even though you may find it fascinating, do not enter into unnecessary conversation with the Spirit. It is quite common for the Spirit to attempt to make a deal with the magician or initiate negotiations on the Spirit's terms. This must be firmly yet courteously resisted at all costs.

You may, if you feel magnanimous, tell the Spirit that after it executes your orders satisfactorily, you will do something nice for it to acknowledge its loyalty; etching its Seal in precious metal or some such honor. But you should take special care to assure the Spirit that as long as it remains loyal and obedient it will share in your good fortune and spiritual success. You will raise it up even as you are raised up.

The License To Depart

After you have given the Spirit its instructions give it permission to go and get to work for you. The classic License to Depart contains words to the effect...

"Depart now and be ready to come whenever I call you up whether it be in the Triangle or not. Go! Go peaceably without causing harm to me or my loved-ones."

After this you free yourself from the *feeling* you experienced when you first sensed the Spirit's presence. The state of mind you aimed for at the beginning of the ceremony must be gone. "Snap out of it!—NOW"

Once you have returned to an objective, "waking consciousness," perform again the Banishing Ritual of the Pentagram and disassemble the Temple. Remove the Seal from the Triangle and place it in the location you have prepared for it.

Then forget the whole thing for as long as you can. The more you can release it from you mind the faster the Spirit can go to work for you.

CHAPTER EIGHT

The Seventy-Two Spirits

T he list of Spirits which follows is from Crowley's original Goetia—which also includes many other prerequisites for evocation. The timing was especially important to the ancient practitioners. Even though we do not wish to discourage any practitioner who wishes to make the observation of the days and hours part of his or her working, the experience of many modern magicians has shown that the Spirits are easily evoked at any hour of the day or night and on any day of the year.

In Crowley's *777* (Weiser, 1986), in columns 155, 157, 159, 161, 163 and 165, he attributed the Seventy-Two Spirits of the Goetia (in pairs, Day/Night) to the Decans of the Zodiac. By doing so, he established a relationship to the small cards of the Tarot and, of course, to the days of the year.

We have included that information along with the traditional attributes of the Spirits in what follows. We caution the reader to remember that these correspondences do not serve to perfectly define each other. For example, the Spirit Bael is attributed to the daylight hours of the first Ten Degrees of Aries, and these degrees are represented in the Tarot by the TWO OF WANDS; but that does not necessarily mean that in all matters Bael is the TWO OF WANDS or that the TWO OF WANDS always represents Bael.

To illustrate how this information could be useful we offer the following example:

A magician is troubled by a personal or magical problem, let's say a misunderstanding with a friend or colleague. He decides to perform a Tarot Divination to get insight into how to proceed to correct the situation. The final card in his Tarot spread is the EIGHT OF SWORDS (Interference). This, in itself, quite accurately describes the situation but does not give him much of a clue as to what to do. But, he notes that the EIGHT OF SWORDS represents the first Ten Degrees of Gemini and that this period is represented (in the daytime) by the seventh Goetic Spirit, AMON, who, among other things, "tells all things past and to come and procures feuds and reconciles controversies between friends." After some thought, he decides to evoke AMON for the purpose of "reconciling the controversy."

It only takes a little imagination to see other applications for these correspondences.

The illustrations of the 72 Spirits that appear below are the work of artist-clairvoyant David P. Wilson who is also a talented and adept Goetic Magician. Over a period of 15 years, he has evoked each of the Spirits at least once, and has recorded some of the most remarkable Goetic experiences we have yet encountered.

But it is very important for you to remember that, because no two people have the same visual-emotional "vocabulary," the images of the Goetic universe will be unique to each of us. When you participate in an evocation you most likely will "see" something entirely different than the images described and illustrated below. Do not think that these sketches are what you *must* see when evoking any particular Spirit. They are intended to serve only as springboards to your imagination.

𝔍ntroduction:
𝔉rom 𝕿he 𝕭oetia

𝕿hese are the 72 Mighty Kings and Princes which King Solomon Commanded into a Vessel of Brass, together with their Legions. Of whom BELIAL, BILETH, ASMODAY, and GAAP, were Chief. And it is to be noted that Solomon did this because of their pride, for he never declared other reason why he thus bound them. And when he had thus bound them up and sealed the Vessel, he by Divine Power chased them all into a deep Lake or Hole in Babylon. And they of Babylon, wondering to see such a thing, they did then go wholly into the Lake, to break the Vessel open, expecting to find great store of Treasure therein. But when they had broken it open, out flew the Chief Spirits immediately, with their Legions following them; and they were all restored to their former places except BELIAL, who entered into a certain Image, and thence gave answers unto those who did offer Sacrifices unto him, and worshiped the Image as their God.

OBSERVATIONS

First, thou shalt know and observe the Moon's age for thy working. The best days be when the Moon Luna is 2, 4, 6, 8, 10, 12, or 14 days old, as Solomon saith; and no other days be profitable. The Seals of the 72 Kings are to be made in Metals. The Chief Kings' in Sol (Gold); Marquises' in Luna (Silver); Dukes' in Venus (Copper); Prelacies' in Jupiter (Tin); Knights' in Saturn (Lead); Presidents' in Mercury (Mercury); Earls' in Venus (Copper) [Crowley's notes suggest Mars (Iron)—Ed.], and Luna (Silver), alike equal, etc.

These 72 Kings are under the Power of AMAYMON, CORSON, ZIMIMAY or ZIMINIAR, and GOAP, who are the Four Great Kings ruling in the Four Quarters, or Cardinal

Points,[11] viz.: East, West, North, and South, and are not to be called forth except it be upon Great Occasions; but are to be Invocated and Commanded to send such or such a Spirit that is under their Power and Rule, as is shown in the following Invocations or Conjurations. And the Chief Kings may be bound from 9 till 12 o'clock at Noon, and from 3 till Sunset; Marquises may be bound from 3 in the afternoon till 9 at Night, and from 9 at Night till Sunrise; Dukes may be bound from Sunrise till Noonday in Clear Weather; Prelates may be bound any hour of the Day; Knights may from Dawning of Day till Sunrise, or from 4 o'clock till Sunset; Presidents may be bound any time, excepting Twilight, at Night, unless the King whom they are under be Invocated; and Counties or Earls any hour of the Day, so it be in Woods, or in any other places whither men resort not, or where no noise is, etc.

Here follows the images of the 72 Spirits and their Seals.

---

[11] These four Great Kings are usually called Oriens, or Uriens, Paymon or Paymonia, Ariton or Egyn, and Amaymon or Amaimon. By the Rabbins they are frequently entitled: Samael, Azazel, Azäel, and Mahazael.

Lucifuge Rofocale
Prime Minister Of Hell

Based upon a seventieth century illustration
in the original *Grand Grimoire*.

𝕭AEL

KING
1°—10° ARIES (day)
March 21—30

TWO OF WANDS   SOL—GOLD

𝕿he First Principal Spirit is called Bael, a King ruling in the East. He can make the Magician invisible. He rules over 66 Legions of Infernal Spirits. He can appear in many forms, sometimes like a cat, sometimes like a toad, and sometimes like a man, and sometimes all these forms at once. He speaks hoarsely.

𝕬GARES

DUKE
10°—20° ARIES (day)
March 31—April 10

THREE OF WANDS   VENUS—COPPER

𝕿he Second Spirit is a Duke called Agreas, or Agares. He is under the power of the East, and comes in the form of an old fair man, riding upon a crocodile, carrying a goshawk upon his fist. He is mild in appearance. He makes them to run that stand still, and brings back runaways. He teaches all languages and tongues. He has the power to destroy dignities both spiritual and temporal, and causes earthquakes. He was of the Order of Virtues. He governs 31 Legions of Spirits.

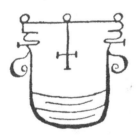

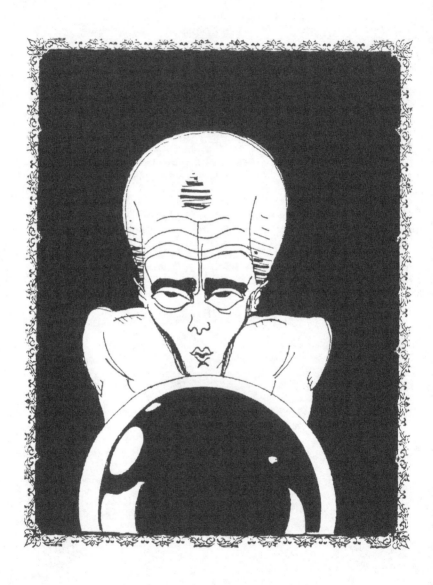

♄ASSAGO

PRINCE
20°—30° ARIES (day)
April 11—20

FOUR OF WANDS   JUPITER—TIN

The Third Spirit is called Vassago and is a Mighty Prince. He is of the same nature as Agares. This Spirit is of a good nature, and his office is to declare things past and to come, and to discover all things hidden or lost. He governs 26 Legions of Spirits.

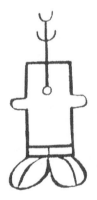

𝕾AMIGINA

MARQUIS
1°—10° Taurus (day)
April 21—30

FIVE OF DISKS   LUNA—SILVER

𝕿he Fourth Spirit is Samigina, or Gamigin, a Great Marquis. He appears in the form of a little horse or ass, and then changes into human shape at the request of the Magician. He speaks with a hoarse voice. He teaches all liberal sciences, and gives account of dead souls that died in sin. He governs 30 Legions of Inferiors.

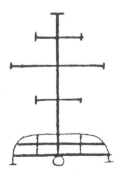

𝔐ARBAS

PRESIDENT
10°—20° Taurus (day)
May 1—10

SIX OF DISKS   MERCURY—MERCURY

The fifth Spirit is Marbas. He is a Great President, and appears at first in the form of a great lion, but afterwards, at the request of the Magician, puts on human form. He answers truthfully concerning things hidden or secret. He causes diseases and cures them. He gives great wisdom and knowledge in mechanical arts and can change men into other shapes. He governs 36 Legions of Spirits.

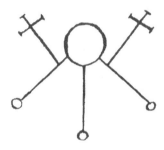

𝔙ALEFOR

DUKE
20°—30° Taurus (day)
May 11—20

SEVEN OF DISKS   VENUS—COPPER

𝕿he Sixth Spirit is Valefor. He is a Mighty Duke, and appears in the shape of a lion with an ass's head, bellowing (or lowing). He is a good Familiar, but tempts the Magician to steal. He governs 10 Legions of Spirits. His Seal is to be worn, whether you will have him for a Familiar or not.

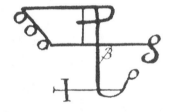

𝔄MON

MARQUIS
1°—10° Gemini (day)
May 21—31

EIGHT OF SWORDS   LUNA—SILVER

The Seventh Spirit is Amon. He is a Marquis great in power, and most stern. He appears like a wolf with a serpent's tail. Out of his mouth vomits flames of fire; but at the command of the Magician he puts on the shape of a man with dog's teeth beset in a head like a raven; or simply like a man with a raven's head. He tells all things past and to come. He procures feuds and reconciles controversies between friends. He governs 40 Legions of Spirits.

𝕭ARBATOS

DUKE
10°—20° Gemini (day)
June 1—10

NINE OF SWORDS   VENUS—COPPER

𝕿he Eighth Spirit is Barbatos. He is a Great Duke, and appears when the Sun is in Sagittarius, with four noble Kings and their companies of great troops. He gives understanding of the singing of birds, and of the voices of other creatures, such as the barking of dogs. He breaks the hidden treasures open that have been laid by the enchantments of Magicians. He is of the Order of Virtues, of which some part he retains still; and he knows all things past, and to come, and conciliates friends and those who are in power. He rules over 30 Legions of Spirits.

$\mathfrak{P}$AIMON

KING
20°—30° Gemini (day)
June 11—20

TEN OF SWORDS   SOL—GOLD

$\mathfrak{T}$he Ninth Spirit in this Order is Paimon, a Great King, and very obedient unto LUCIFER. He appears in the form of a man sitting upon a dromedary with a most glorious crown upon his head. Before him march an host of Spirits, like men with trumpets and cymbals, and all other sorts of musical instruments. He has a great voice, and roars at his first coming, and his speech is such that the Magician will not be able to understand him unless compelled. He can teach all arts and sciences, and other secret things. He can reveal to you what the Earth is, and what holds it up in the Waters; and what mind is, and where it is; or any other thing you may desire to know. He gives Dignity, and confirms the same. He binds or makes any man subject unto the Magician if he so desire it. He gives good Familiars, who can teach all arts. He is to be observed towards the West. He is of the Order of Dominations.(Dominions) He has under him 200 Legions of Spirits, and part of them are of the Order of Angels, and the other part of Potentates. Now if you call this Spirit Paimon alone, you must make him some offering; and there will attend him two Kings called LABAL and ABALIM, and also other Spirits who are of the Order of Potentates in his Host, and 25 Legions. And those Spirits who are subject unto them are not always with them unless the Magician compels them.

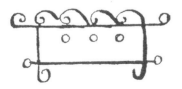

𝕭UER

PRESIDENT
1°—10° Cancer (day)
June 21—July 1

TWO OF CUPS   MERCURY—MERCURY

𝕿he Tenth Spirit is Buer, a Great President. He appears as an archer when the Sun is in Sagittarius. He teaches philosophy, both moral and natural, and the art of logic, also the Virtues of all herbs and plants. He heals all distempers in man, and gives good Familiars. He governs 50 Legions of Spirits.

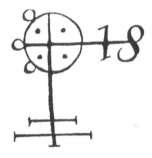

ⒼUSION

DUKE
10°—20° Cancer (day)
July 2—11

THREE OF CUPS   VENUS—COPPER

The Eleventh Spirit in order is a Great and Strong Duke, called Gusion. He appears like a xenopilus (blue headed or strange headed creature). He tells all things, past, present, and to come, and shows the meaning and resolution of all questions you may ask. He conciliates and reconciles friendships, and gives honor and dignity unto any. He rules over 40 Legions of Spirits.

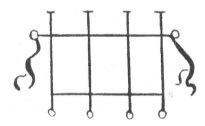

$\mathfrak{S}$ITRI

PRINCE
20°—30° Cancer (day)
July 12—21

FOUR OF CUPS   JUPITER—TIN

The Twelfth Spirit is Sitri. He is a Great Prince, and appears at first with a Leopard's head and the Wings of a Gryphon, but after the command of the Magician he assumes human form, and that very beautiful. He enflames men with women's love, and women with men's love; and causes them also to show themselves naked if so desired. He governs 60 Legions of Spirits.

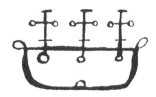

ℬELETH

KING
1°—10° Leo (day)
July 22—August 1

FIVE OF WANDS   SOL—GOLD

𝕿he Thirteenth Spirit is called Beleth (or Bileth, or Bilet). He is a terrible and Mighty King. He rides upon a pale horse. Trumpets and other kinds of musical instruments play before him. He is very furious at his first appearance, that is, while the Exorcist lays his courage; for to do this he must hold a Hazel Wand in his hand, striking it out towards the South and East Quarters, make a Triangle, without the Circle, and then command him into it by the Bonds and Charges of Spirits. And if he does not enter into the Triangle, at your threats, rehearse the Bonds and Charms before him, and then he will yield obedience and come into it, and do what he is commanded by the Exorcist. Yet the Magician must receive him courteously because he is a Great King, and do homage unto him, as the Kings and Princes do that attend upon him. And you must have always a Silver Ring on the middle finger of your left hand held against your face as is done before AMAYMON, to be protected from the flaming breath of the enraged Spirit. This Great King Beleth causes all the love that may be, both of men and of women, until the Master Exorcist has had his desire fulfilled. He is of the Order of Powers, and he governs 85 Legions of Spirits.

𝔏ERAJE

MARQUIS
10°—20° Leo (day)
August 2—11

SIX OF WANDS   LUNA—SILVER

𝕿he Fourteenth Spirit is called Leraje (or Leraikha or Leraie).
He is a Marquis great in power. He appears, when the sun is in
Sagittarius, in the likeness of an archer clad in green, carrying
a bow and quiver. He causes great battles and contests; and
makes wounds to putrefy that are made with arrows by archers.
He governs 30 Legions of Spirits.

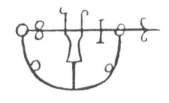

𝕰LIGOS

DUKE
20°—30° Leo (day)
August 12—22

SEVEN OF WANDS   VENUS—COPPER

𝕿he Fifteenth Spirit in Order is Eligos, a Great Duke, and appears in the form of a handsome Knight, carrying a lance, an ensign, and a serpent. He discovers hidden things, and knows things to come; and of wars, and how the soldiers will or shall meet. He causes the love of Lords and great persons. He governs 60 Legions of Spirits.

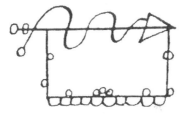

ℨEPAR

DUKE
1°—10° Virgo (day)
August 23—September 1

EIGHT OF DISKS   VENUS—COPPER

The Sixteenth Spirit is Zepar. He is a Great Duke, and appears in red apparel and armour, like a soldier. His office is to cause women to love men, and to bring them together in love. He also makes them barren. He governs 26 Legions of Inferior Spirits.

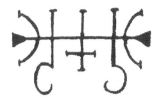

𝔅OTIS

PRESIDENT
10°—20° Virgo (day)
September 2—11

NINE OF DISKS   MERCURY—MERCURY

𝕿he Seventeenth Spirit is Botis, a Great President, and an Earl. He appears at the first in the form of an ugly viper, then at the command of the Magician he assumes human form with great teeth, and two horns, carrying a bright and sharp sword in his hand. He tells all things past, and to come, and reconciles friends and foes. He rules over 60 Legions of Spirits.

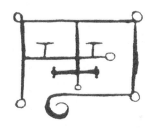

BATHIN

DUKE
20°—30° Virgo (day)
September 12—22

TEN OF DISKS   VENUS—COPPER

The Eighteenth Spirit is Bathin. He is a Mighty and Strong Duke, and appears like a strong man with the tail of a serpent, sitting upon a pale-colored horse or ass. He knows the virtues of herbs and precious stones and can transport men suddenly from one country to another. He rules over 30 Legions of Spirits.

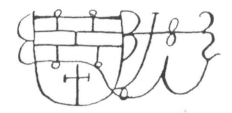

$\mathfrak{S}$ALLOS

DUKE
1°—10° Libra (day)
September 23—October 2

TWO OF SWORDS   VENUS—COPPER

$\mathfrak{T}$he Nineteenth Spirit is Sallos (or Saleos). He is a Great and Mighty Duke, and appears in the form of a gallant soldier riding on a crocodile, with a Ducal crown on his head. He is very peaceable. He causes the love of women to men, and of men to women; and governs 30 Legions of Spirits.

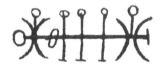

℘URSON

KING
10°—20° Libra (day)
October 3—12

THREE OF SWORDS   SOL—GOLD

The Twentieth Spirit is Purson, a Great King. His appearing is comely, like a man with a lion's face, carrying a cruel viper in his hand, and riding upon a bear. Going before him are many trumpets sounding. He knows all things hidden, and can discover treasure, and tell all things past, present, and to come. He can take either a human or aerial body and answers truthfully all questions of an Earthly nature both secret and Divine, and of the creation of the world. He brings good Familiars, and he governs 22 Legions of Spirits, partly of the Order of Virtues and partly of the Order of Thrones.

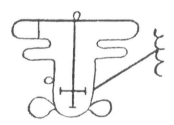

𝕸arax

EARL/PRESIDENT
20°—30° Libra (day)
October 13—22

FOUR OF SWORDS   MARS—IRON
                                  MERCURY—MERCURY

The Twenty-first Spirit is Marax. (Sometimes spelled Morax) He is a Great Earl and President. He appears like a great bull with a man's face. His office is to make the Magician very knowing in astronomy, and all other liberal sciences; also he can give good and wise Familiars, knowing the virtues of herbs and precious stones. He governs 30 Legions of Spirits.

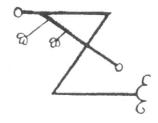

𝕴pos

EARL/PRINCE
1°—10° Scorpio (day)
October 23—November 1

FIVE OF CUPS   MARS—IRON
                                      JUPITER—TIN

The Twenty-second Spirit is Ipos. He is an Earl, and a Mighty Prince, and appears in the form of an angel with a lion's head, and a goose's foot, and hare's tail. He knows all things past, present, and to come. He makes men witty and bold. He governs 36 Legions of Spirits.

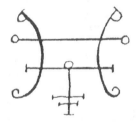

𝕬IM

DUKE

10°—20° Scorpio (day)
November 2—12

SIX OF CUPS   VENUS—COPPER

𝕿he Twenty-third Spirit is Aim. He is a Great Strong Duke. He appears in the form of a very handsome man in body, but with three heads; the first, like a serpent, the second like a man having two Stars on his forehead, the third like a calf. He rides on a viper, carrying a firebrand in his hand, with this he sets fire to cities, castles, and great Places. He makes one witty in all manner of ways, and gives true answers concerning private matters. He governs 26 Legions of Inferior Spirits.

𝔑ABERIUS

MARQUIS
20°—30° Scorpio (day)
November 13—22

SEVEN OF CUPS   LUNA—SILVER

The Twenty-fourth Spirit is Naberius. He is a most Valiant Marquis, and shows in the form of a black crane fluttering about the Circle, and when he speaks it is with a hoarse voice. He makes men cunning in all arts and sciences, but especially in the art of rhetoric. He restores lost Dignities and Honors. He governs 19 Legions of Spirits.

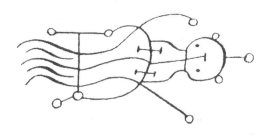

ⒼLASYA-ⓁABOLAS

PRESIDENT/EARL
1°—10° Sagittarius (day)
November 23—December 2

EIGHT OF WANDS   MERCURY—MERCURY
                                  MARS—IRON

𝕿he Twenty-fifth Spirit is Glasya-Labolas. He is a Mighty President and Earl, and shows himself in the form of a dog with wings like a gryphon. He teaches all arts and sciences in an instant, and is an author of bloodshed and manslaughter. He teaches all things past, and to come. If desired he causes the love both of friends and of foes. He can make a man Invisible. And he has under his command 36 Legions of Spirits.

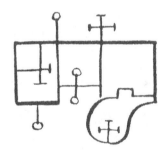

𝕭UNÉ

DUKE

10°—20° Sagittarius (day)
December 3—12

NINE OF WANDS   VENUS—COPPER

𝕿he Twenty-sixth Spirit is Buné (or Bimé or Bim). He is a Strong, Great and Mighty Duke. He appears in the form of a dragon with three heads, one like a dog, one like a gryphon, and one like a man. He speaks with a high and comely voice. He changes the burial places of the dead, and causes the Spirits which are under him to gather together upon your sepulchres. He gives riches and makes the Magician wise and eloquent. He gives truthful answers unto demands. He governs 30 Legions of Spirits.

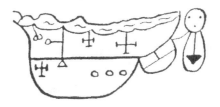

Ronové

MARQUIS/EARL
20°—30° Sagittarius (day)
December 13—21

TEN OF WANDS   LUNA—SILVER
                                      MARS—IRON

The Twenty-seventh Spirit is Ronové. He is a Marquis and Great Earl. He appears in the form of a monster. He teaches the art of rhetoric very well, and gives good servants, knowledge of tongues, and favors with friends or foes. There are under his command 19 Legions of Spirits.

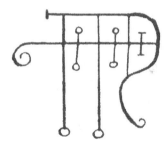

𝔅ERITH

DUKE
1°—10° Capricorn (day)
December 22—30

TWO OF DISKS   VENUS—COPPER

𝕿he Twenty-eighth Spirit in Order, as Solomon bound them, is named Berith. He is a Mighty, Great, and Terrible Duke. He has two other Names given unto him by men of later times, viz: BEALE, or BEAL, and BOFRY or BOLFRY. He appears in the Form of a soldier with red clothing, riding upon a red horse, and having a crown of gold upon his head. He gives true answers, past, present, and to come. You must make use of a Ring in calling him forth, as is before spoken of regarding Beleth. He can turn all metals into gold. He can give Dignities, and can confirm them unto man. He speaks with a very clear and subtle voice. Notwithstanding what is said above it is written he is a great liar, and not to be trusted. He governs 26 Legions of Spirits.

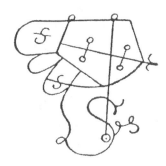

𝕬STAROTH

DUKE
10°—20° Capricorn (day)
December 31—January 9

THREE OF DISKS   VENUS—COPPER

𝕿he Twenty-ninth Spirit is Astaroth. He is a Mighty, Strong Duke, and appears in the form of a hurtful [some texts read *un*hurtful—Ed.] angel riding on an infernal beast like a dragon, and carrying in his right hand a viper. You must in no wise let him approach too near unto you, lest he do you damage by his noisome breath. Wherefore the Magician must hold the Magical Ring near his face, and that will defend him. He gives true answers of things past, present, and to come, and can discover all secrets. He will declare wittingly how the Spirits fell, if desired, and the reason of his own fall. He can make men wonderfully knowing in all liberal sciences. He rules 40 Legions of Spirits.

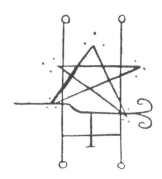

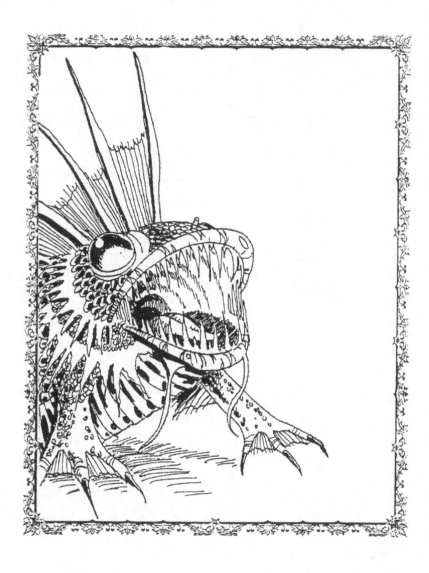

𝔉ORNEUS

MARQUIS
20°—30° Capricorn (day)
January 10—19

FOUR OF DISKS   LUNA—SILVER

𝕿he Thirtieth Spirit is Forneus. He is a Mighty and Great Marquis, and appears in the form of a great sea-monster. He teaches and makes men wonderfully knowledgeable in the art of rhetoric. He causes men to have a good name, and to have the knowledge and understanding of tongues. He makes one to be beloved of his foes as well as of his friends. He governs 29 Legions of Spirits, partly of the Order of Thrones, and partly of that of Angels.

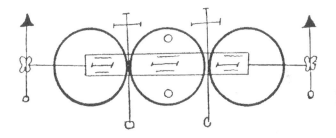

𝔉ORAS

PRESIDENT
1°—10° Aquarius (day)
January 20—29

FIVE OF SWORDS   MERCURY—MERCURY

The Thirty-first Spirit is Foras. He is a Mighty President, and appears in the form of a strong man in human shape. He can give the understanding to men how they may know the virtues of all Herbs and Precious Stones. He teaches the Arts of Logic and ethics in all their parts. If desired he makes men invisible, (some texts say "invincible") and to live long, and to be eloquent. He can discover Treasures and recover things Lost. He rules over 29 Legions of Spirits

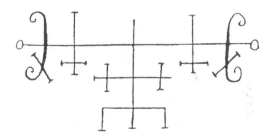

𝔄SMODAY

KING
10°—20° Aquarius (day)
January 30—February 8

SIX OF SWORDS   SOL—GOLD

𝕿he Thirty-second Spirit is Asmoday, or Asmodai. He is a Great King, strong, and powerful. He appears with three heads. The first is like a bull, the second like a man, and the third like a ram; he also has the tail of a serpent, and from his mouth issue flames of fire. His feet are webbed like those of a goose. He sits upon an infernal dragon, and bears in his hand a lance with a banner. He is first and choicest under the power of AMAYMON, he goes before all other. When the Exorcist has a mind to call him, let it be abroad, and let him stand on his feet all the time of action, with his cap or head-dress off; for if it be on, AMAYMON will deceive him and cause all his actions to be betrayed. But as soon as the Exorcist sees Asmoday in the aforesaid shape, he shall call him by his name, saying: "Are you Asmoday?" and he will not deny it, and eventually he will bow down unto the ground. He gives the Ring of Virtues; he teaches the arts of arithmetic, astronomy, geometry, and all handicrafts absolutely. He gives true and full answers unto your demands. He makes one invincible. He shows the place where treasures lie, and guards it. He, among the Legions of AMAYMON governs 72 Legions of Inferior Spirits.

⅁AAP

PRESIDENT/PRINCE
20°—30° Aquarius (day)
February 9—18

SEVEN OF SWORDS   MERCURY—MERCURY
                                   JUPITER—TIN

The Thirty-third Spirit is Gaap. He is a Great President and a Mighty Prince. He appears when the Sun is in some of the Southern Signs, in a human form, going before four great and mighty Kings, as if he were a guide to conduct them along on their way. His office is to make men insensible or ignorant. But he can also make one knowledgeable in philosophy and liberal sciences. He can cause love or hatred, also he can teach you to consecrate those things that belong to the Dominion of AMAYMON his King. He can deliver Familiars out of the custody of other Magicians, and answer truly and perfectly of things past, present, and to come. He can carry and re-carry men very speedily from one kingdom to another, at the will and pleasure of the Exorcist. He rules over 66 Legions of Spirits, and he was of the Order of Potentates.

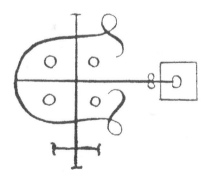

𝔉URFUR

EARL
1°—10° Pisces (day)
February 19—28

EIGHT OF CUPS   MARS—IRON

The Thirty-fourth Spirit is Furfur. He is a Great and Mighty Earl, appearing in the form of an hart with a fiery tail. He never speaks the truth unless he is compelled, or brought up within the Triangle, Being therein, he will take upon himself the form of an angel. Being bidden, he speaks with a hoarse voice. Also he will wittingly urge love between man and woman. He can raise lightnings and thunders, blasts, and great tempestuous storms. And he gives true answers both of things secret and Divine, if commanded. He rules over 26 Legions of Spirits.

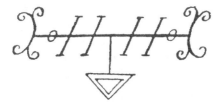

𝕸ARCHOSIAS

MARQUIS
10°—20° Pisces (day)
March 1—10

NINE OF CUPS   LUNA—SILVER

𝕿he Thirty-fifth Spirit is Marchosias. He is a Great and Mighty Marquis, appearing at first in the form of a wolf or ox having gryphon's wings, and a serpent's tail, and vomiting fire out of his mouth. But after a time, at the command of the Exorcist he assumes the shape of a man. He is a strong fighter. He was of the Order of Dominations. He governs 30 Legions of Spirits. He told his Chief, who was Solomon, that after 1,200 years he had hopes to return unto the Seventh Throne.

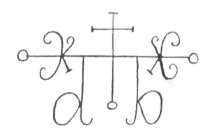

$\mathfrak{S}$TOLAS

PRINCE
20°—30° Pisces (day)
March 11—20

TEN OF CUPS   JUPITER—TIN

The Thirty-sixth Spirit is Stolas, or Stolos. He is a Great and Powerful Prince, appearing in the shape of a mighty raven at first before the Exorcist; but after he takes the image of a man. He teaches the art of astronomy, and the virtues of herbs and precious stones. He governs 26 Legions of Spirits.

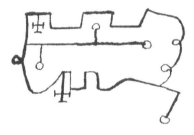

ℙHENEX

MARQUIS
1°—10° ARIES (night)
March 21—30

TWO OF WANDS   LUNA—SILVER

𝕿he Thirty-seventh Spirit is Phenex (or Pheynix). He is a Great Marquis, and appears like the bird Phoenix, having the voice of a child. He sings many sweet notes before the Magician which he must not regard, but eventually he must require him to assume human form. Then if required he will speak marvelously of all wonderful sciences. He is an excellent poet and he will be willing to perform your requests. He has hopes also to return to the Seventh Throne after 1,200 years more, as he said unto Solomon. He governs 20 Legions of Spirits.

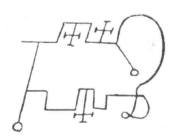

ḢALPHAS

EARL
10°—20° ARIES (night)
March 31—April 10

THREE OF WANDS   MARS—IRON

The Thirty-eighth Spirit is Halphas, or Malthus (or Malthas). He is a Great Earl, and appears in the form of a stock-dove. He speaks with a hoarse voice. His office is to build up towers, and to furnish them with ammunition and weapons, and to send warriors to places appointed. He rules over 26 Legions of Spirits.

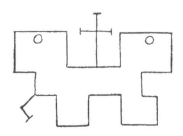

𝔐ALPHAS

PRESIDENT
20°—30° ARIES (night)
April 11—20

FOUR OF WANDS   MERCURY—MERCURY

The Thirty-ninth Spirit is Malphas. He is a Mighty and Powerful President. He appears at first like a crow, but after he will put on human shape at the request of the Exorcist, and speak with a hoarse Voice. He can build houses and high towers, and can inform you of your enemies' desires and thoughts, and that which they have done. He gives good Familiars. If you make a sacrifice unto him he will receive it kindly and willingly, but he will deceive him that does it. He governs 40 Legions of Spirits.

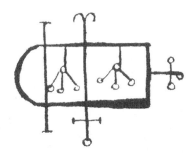

𝕽AUM

EARL
1°—10° Taurus (night)
April 21—30

FIVE OF DISKS   MARS—IRON

𝕿he Fortieth Spirit is Raum. He is a Great Earl; and appears at first in the form of a crow, but after the command of the Exorcist he puts on human shape. His office is to steal treasures out King's houses, and to carry it where he is commanded, and to destroy cities and Dignities of men, and to tell all things, past, and what is, and what will be; and to cause love between friends and foes. He was of the Order of Thrones. He governs 30 Legions of Spirits.

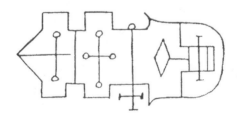

𝔉OCALOR

DUKE
10°—20° Taurus (night)
May 1—10

SIX OF DISKS   VENUS—COPPER

𝕿he Forty-first Spirit is Focalor, or Forcalor, or Furcalor. He is a strong and Mighty Duke. He appears in the form of a man with gryphon's wings. His office is to slay men, and to drown them in the waters, and to overthrow ships of war, for he has power over both winds and seas; but he will not hurt any man or thing if he is commanded to the contrary by the Exorcist. He also has hopes to return to the Seventh Throne after 1,000 years. He governs 30 Legions of Spirits.

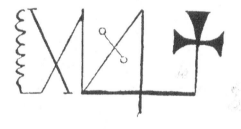

𝔙EPAR

DUKE
20°—30° Taurus (night)
May 11—20

SEVEN OF DISKS   VENUS—COPPER

𝕿he Forty-second Spirit is Vapar, or Vephar. She is a Duke great and strong, and appears like a Mermaid. Her office is to govern the waters, and to guide ships laden with arms, armour, and ammunition, etc. At the request of the Exorcist she can cause the seas to be stormy and to appear full of ships. Also she makes men to die in three days by putrefying wounds or sores causing worms to breed in them. She governs 29 Legions of Spirits.

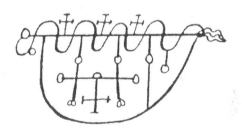

ꙄABNOCK

MARQUIS
1°—10° Gemini (night)
May 21—31

EIGHT OF SWORDS   LUNA—SILVER

The Forty-third Spirit, as King Solomon commanded them into the Vessel of Brass, is called Sabnock, or Savnok. He is a Marquis, mighty, great and strong, appearing in the form of an armed soldier with a lion's head, riding on a pale-colored horse. His office is to build high towers, castles and cities, and to furnish them with armour, etc. Also he can afflict men for many days with wounds and with sores rotten and full of worms. He gives good Familiars and commands 50 Legions of Spirits.

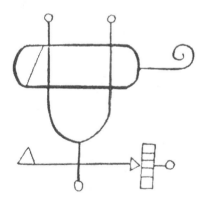

ℬHAX

MARQUIS
10°—20° Gemini (night)
June 1—10

NINE OF SWORDS   LUNA—SILVER

The Forty-fourth Spirit is Shax, or Shaz (or Shass). He is a Great Marquis and appears in the form of a stock-dove, speaking with a voice hoarse, but yet subtle. His office is to take away the sight, hearing, or understanding of any man or woman at the command of the Exorcist; and to steal money out of the houses of Kings, and to carry it again in 1,200 years. If commanded he will fetch horses at the request of the Exorcist, or any other thing. But he must first be commanded into a Triangle, or else he will deceive him, and tell him many lies. He can discover all things that are hidden, and not kept by wicked spirits. He gives good Familiars, sometimes. He governs 30 Legions of Spirits.

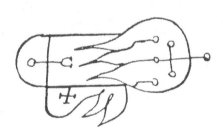

♆INÉ

KING/EARL
20°—30° Gemini (night)
June 11—20

TEN OF SWORDS   SOL—GOLD
                                                 MARS—IRON

The Forty-fifth Spirit is Viné, or Vinea. He is a Great King, and an Earl; and appears in the form of a lion, (or having the head of a lion), riding upon a black horse, and bearing a viper in his hand. His office is to discover things hidden, witches, wizards, and things present, past, and to come. He, at the command of the Exorcist will build towers, overthrow great stone walls, and make the waters rough with storms. He governs 36 Legions of Spirits.

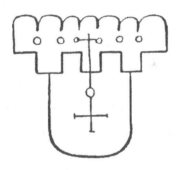

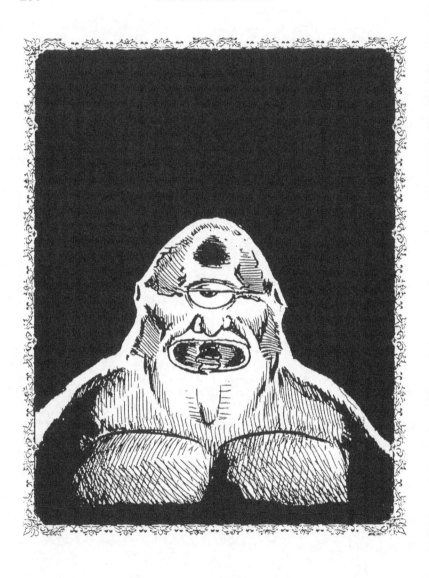

BIFRONS

EARL
1°—10° Cancer (night)
June 21—July 1

TWO OF CUPS   MARS—IRON

The Forty-sixth Spirit is called Bifrons, or Bifrous, or Bifrovs. He is an Earl, and appears in the form of a monster; but after a while, at the command of the Exorcist, he assumes the shape of a Man. His office is to make one knowledgeable in astrology, geometry, and other arts and sciences. He teaches the virtues of precious stones and woods. He changes dead bodies, and puts them in another place; also he lights seeming candles upon the graves of the dead. He has under his command 60 Legions of Spirits.

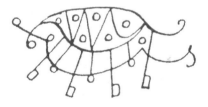

⅌VALL

DUKE
10°—20° Cancer (night)
July 2—11

THREE OF CUPS   VENUS—COPPER

The Forty-seventh Spirit is Uvall, or Vual, or Voval. He is a Duke great mighty and strong. He appears in the form of a mighty dromedary at the first, but after a while at the command of the Exorcist he puts on human shape, and speaks the Egyptian tongue, but not perfectly. His Office is to procure the love of women, and to tell things past, present, and to come. He also procures friendship between friends and foes. He was of the Order of Potentates or Powers. He governs 37 Legions of Spirits.

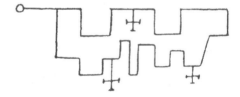

ℌAAGENTI

PRESIDENT
20°—30° Cancer (night)
July 12—21

FOUR OF CUPS   MERCURY—MERCURY

The Forty-eighth Spirit is Haagenti. He is a President, appearing in the form of a mighty bull with gryphon's wings. This is at first, but after, at the command of the Exorcist he puts on human shape. His office is to make men wise, and to instruct them in divers things; also to transmute all metals into gold; and to change wine into water, and water into wine. He governs 33 Legions of Spirits.

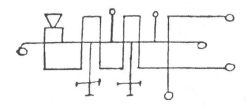

CROCELL

DUKE
1°—10° Leo (night)
July 22—August 1

FIVE OF WANDS   VENUS—COPPER

The Forty-ninth Spirit is Crocell, or Crokel. He appears in the form of an angel. He is a Great and Strong Duke, speaking mystically of hidden things. He teaches the art of geometry and the liberal sciences. He, at the command of the Exorcist, will produce great noises like the rushing of many waters, although there be none. He warms waters, and discovers baths. He was of the Order of Potentates, or Powers, before his fall, as he declared unto the King Solomon. He governs 48 Legions of Spirits.

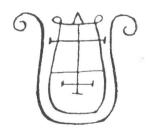

𝔉URCAS

KNIGHT
10°—20° Leo (night)
August 2—11

SIX OF WANDS   SATURN—LEAD

𝕿he Fiftieth Spirit is Furcas. He is a Knight, and appears in the form of a cruel old man with a long beard and a hoary head, riding upon a pale-colored horse, with a sharp weapon in his hand. His office is to teach the arts of philosophy, astrology, rhetoric, logic, cheiromancy, and pyromancy, in all their parts, and perfectly. He has under his Power 20 Legions of Spirits.

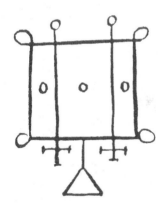

ᴮALAM

KING
20°—30° Leo (night)
August 12—22

SEVEN OF WANDS   SOL—GOLD

The Fifty-first Spirit is Balam or Balaam. He is a terrible, Great, and Powerful King. He appears with three heads: the first is like that of a bull; the second is like that of a man; the third is like that of a ram. He has the tail of a serpent, and flaming eyes. He rides upon a furious bear, and carries a goshawk upon his fist. He speaks with a hoarse voice, giving true answers of things past, present, and to come. He makes men invisible, and also to be witty. He governs 40 Legions of Spirits.

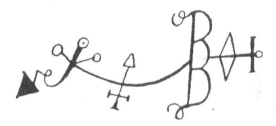

ᴀLLOCES

DUKE
1°—10° Virgo (night)
August 23—September 1

EIGHT OF DISKS   VENUS—COPPER

The Fifty-second Spirit is Alloces, or Alocas. He is a Duke, great, mighty, and strong, appearing in the form of a soldier or warrior riding upon a great horse. His face is like that of a lion, very red, and having flaming eyes. His speech is hoarse and very boisterous. His office is to teach the art of astronomy, and all the liberal sciences. He brings good Familiars; also he rules over 36 Legions of Spirits.

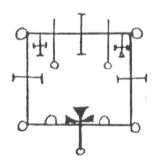

Camio

PRESIDENT
10°—20° Virgo (night)
September 2—11

NINE OF DISKS   MERCURY—MERCURY

The Fifty-third Spirit is Camio, or Caim. He is a Great President, and appears in the form of the bird called a thrush at first, but afterwards he puts on the shape of a man carrying in his hand a sharp sword. He seems to answer in burning ashes, or in coals of fire. He is a good disputer. His office is to give unto men the understanding of all birds, lowing of bullocks, barking of dogs, and other creatures; and also of the voice of the waters. He gives true answers of things to come. He was of the Order of angels, but now rules over 30 Legions of Spirits Infernal.

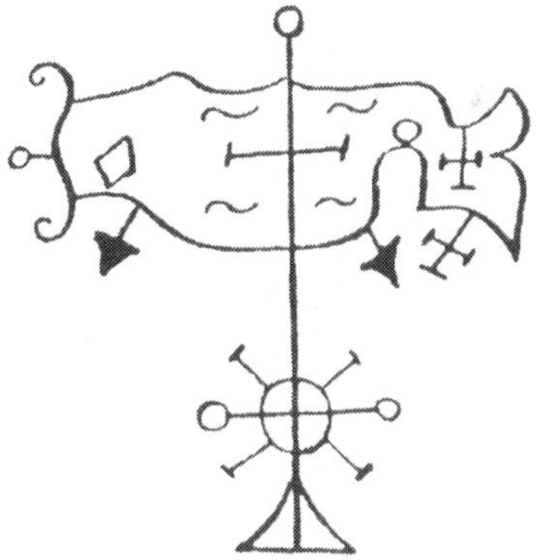

𝔐urmur

DUKE/EARL
20°—30° Virgo (night)
September 12—22

TEN OF DISKS   VENUS—COPPER
                                            MARS—IRON

The Fifty-fourth Spirit is called Murmur, or Murmus, or
Murmux. He is a Great Duke, and an Earl; and appears in the
form of a warrior riding upon a gryphon, with a Ducal crown
upon his head. There go before him those his ministers with
great trumpets sounding. His office is to teach philosophy
perfectly, and to constrain souls deceased to come before the
Exorcist to answer those questions which he may wish to put to
them. He was partly of the Order of Thrones, and partly of that
of Angels. He now rules 30 Legions of Spirits.

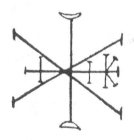

⊕ROBAS

PRINCE
1°—10° Libra (night)
September 23—October 2

TWO OF SWORDS   JUPITER—TIN

The Fifty-fifth Spirit is Orobas. He is a Great and Mighty Prince, appearing at first like a horse; but after the command of the Exorcist he puts on the image of a man. His office is to discover all things past, present, and to come; also to give Dignities, and Prelacies, and the favour of friends and of foes. He gives true answers of divinity, and of the creation of the world. He is very faithful unto the Exorcist, and will not allow him to be tempted of any Spirit. He governs 20 Legions of Spirits.

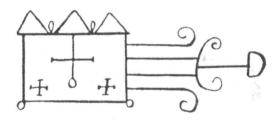

ⒼREMORY

DUKE
10°—20° Libra (night)
October 3—12

THREE OF SWORDS   VENUS—COPPER

Ⓣhe Fifty-sixth Spirit is Gremory, or Gamori. She is a Strong and Powerful Duke, and appears in the form of a beautiful woman, with a Duchess's crown tied about her waist, and riding on a great camel. Her office is to tell of all things past, present, and to come; and of hidden treasures, and what they lie in; and to procure the love of women both young and old. She governs 26 Legions of Spirits.

Ⓞsé

PRESIDENT
20°—30° Libra (night)
October 13—22

FOUR OF SWORDS   MERCURY—MERCURY

The Fifty-seventh Spirit is Osé, Oso or Voso. He is a Great President, and appears at first like a leopard, but after a little time he puts on the shape of a man. His office is to make one cunning in the liberal sciences, and to give true answers of Divine and secret things; also to change a man into any shape that the Exorcist pleases, so that he that is so changed will not think any other thing than that he is in reality that creature or thing he is changed into. He governs 30 Legions of Spirits.

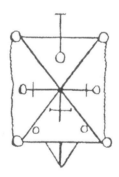

$\mathfrak{A}$MY

PRESIDENT
1°—10° Scorpio (night)
October 23—November 1

FIVE OF CUPS   MERCURY—MERCURY

$\mathfrak{T}$he Fifty-eighth Spirit is Amy or Avnas. He is a Great President, and appears at first in the form of a flaming fire; but after a while he puts on the shape of a man. His office is to make one wonderfully knowledgeable in astrology and all the liberal sciences. He gives good Familiars, and can betray treasure that is kept by Spirits. He governs 36 Legions of Spirits.

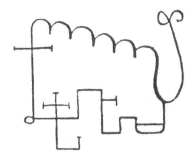

⦾RIAX

MARQUIS
10°—20° Scorpio (night)
November 2—12

SIX OF CUPS   LUNA—SILVER

The Fifty-ninth Spirit is Oriax, or Orias. He is a Great Marquis, and appears with the face of a lion, riding upon a mighty and strong horse with a serpent's tail; and he holds in his right hand two great serpents hissing. His office is to teach the virtues of the stars, and to know the mansions of the planets, and how to understand their virtues. He also transforms men, and he gives Dignities, Prelacies, and confirmation thereof; also favor with friends and with foes. He governs 30 Legions of Spirits.

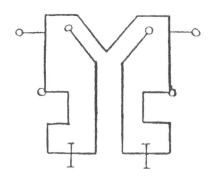

ꝦAPULA

DUKE
20°—30° Scorpio (night)
November 13—22

SEVEN OF CUPS   VENUS—COPPER

The Sixtieth Spirit is Vapula, or Naphula. She is a Duke great, mighty, and strong; appearing in the Form of a Lion with Gryphon's Wings. Her Office is to make men knowledgeable in all handicrafts and professions, also in philosophy, and other sciences. She governs 36 Legions of Spirits.

ẐAGAN

KING/PRESIDENT
1°—10° Sagittarius (night)
November 23—December 2

EIGHT OF WANDS   SOL—GOLD
                            MERCURY—MERCURY

𝕿he Sixty-first Spirit is Zagan. He is a Great King and President, appearing at first in the form of a bull with gryphon's wings; but after a while he puts on human shape. He makes men witty. He can turn wine into water, and blood into wine, also Water into wine. He can turn all metals into coin of the dominion that metal is of. He can even make fools wise. He governs 33 Legions of Spirits.

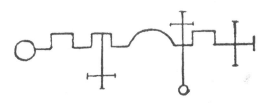

Ᵹolac

PRESIDENT
10°—20° Sagittarius (night)
December 3—12

NINE OF WANDS   MERCURY—MERCURY

The Sixty-second Spirit is Volac, or Valak, or Valu, or Ualac. He is a President mighty and great, and appears like a child with angel's wings, riding on a two-headed dragon. His office is to give true answers of hidden treasures, and to tell where serpents may be seen. The which he will bring to the Magician without any force or strength being by him employed. He governs 38 Legions of Spirits.

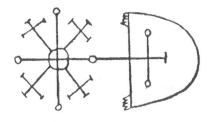

ᴀNDRAS

MARQUIS
20°—30° Sagittarius (night)
December 13—21

TEN OF WANDS   LUNA—SILVER

The Sixty-third Spirit is Andras. He is a Great Marquis, appearing in the form of an angel with a head like a black night raven, riding upon a strong black wolf, and having a sharp and bright sword flourished aloft in his hand. His office is to sow discords. If the Exorcist have not a care, he will slay both him and his fellows. He governs 30 Legions of Spirits.

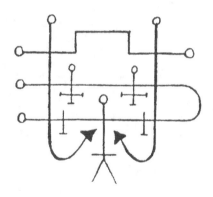

𝕳AURES

DUKE
1°—10° Capricorn (night)
December 22—30

TWO OF DISKS   VENUS—COPPER

The Sixty-fourth Spirit is Haures, or Hauras, or Havres, or Flauros. He is a Great Duke, and appears at first like a leopard, mighty, terrible, and strong, but after a while, at the command of the Exorcist, he puts on human shape with eyes flaming and fiery, and a most terrible countenance. He gives true answers of all things, present, past, and to come. But if he is not commanded into a Triangle, he will lie in all these things, and deceive and beguile the Exorcist in these things. He will, lastly, talk of the creation of the world, and of Divinity, and of how he and other spirits fell. He destroys and burns up those who be the enemies of the Exorcist should he so desire it; also he will not suffer him to be tempted by any other Spirit or otherwise. He governs 36 Legions of Spirits.

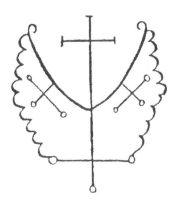

ANDREALPHUS

MARQUIS
10°—20° Capricorn (night)
December 31—January 9

THREE OF DISKS   LUNA—SILVER

The Sixty-fifth Spirit is Andrealphus. He is a Mighty Marquis, appearing at first in the form of a peacock, with great noises. But after a time he puts on Human shape. He can teach geometry perfectly. He makes men very subtle therein; and in all things pertaining unto Mensuration or Astronomy. He can transform a Man into the Likeness of a Bird. He governs 30 Legions of Infernal Spirits.

Cimejes

MARQUIS
20°—30° Capricorn (night)
January 10—19

FOUR OF DISKS   LUNA—SILVER

The Sixty-sixth Spirit is Cimejes, or Cimeies, or Kimaris. He is a Marquis, mighty, great, strong and powerful, appearing like a valiant warrior riding upon a handsome black horse. He rules over all Spirits in the parts of Africa. His office is to teach perfectly grammar, logic, rhetoric, and to discover things lost or hidden, and treasures. He governs 20 Legions of Infernals.

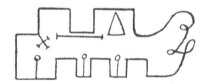

𝔄MDUSIAS

DUKE
1°—10° Aquarius (night)
January 20—29

FIVE OF SWORDS　　　　　　　　VENUS—COPPER

𝕿he Sixty-seventh Spirit is Amdusias, or Amdukias. He is a Great and Strong Duke, appearing at first like a Unicorn, but at the request of the Exorcist he stands before him in Human Shape, causing Trumpets, and all manner of Musical Instruments to be heard, but not soon or immediately. Also he can cause Trees to bend and incline according to the Exorcist's Will. He gives Excellent Familiars. He governs 29 Legions of Spirits.

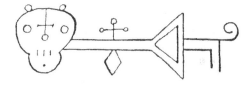

𝕭ELIAL

KING
10°—20° Aquarius (night)
January 30—February 8

SIX OF SWORDS   SOL—GOLD

𝕿he Sixty-eighth Spirit is Belial. He is a mighty and a Powerful King, and was created next after LUCIFER. He appears in the form of a beautiful angel sitting in a chariot of fire. He speaks with a comely Voice, and declares that he fell first from among the worthier sort, that were before Michael, and other heavenly angels. His office is to distribute Presentations and Senatorships, etc., and to cause favour of friends and of foes. He gives excellent Familiars, and governs 50 Legions of Spirits. Note well that this King Belial must have offerings, sacrifices and gifts presented unto him by the Exorcist, or else he will not give true answers unto his demands. But then he tarries not one hour in the truth, unless he be constrained by Divine Power.

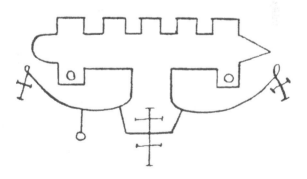

ᴅECARABIA

MARQUIS
20°—30° Aquarius (night)
February 9—18

SEVEN OF SWORDS   LUNA—SILVER

The Sixty-ninth Spirit is Decarabia. He is a Great Marquis. He appears in the form of a star in a pentacle at first; but after, at the command of the Exorcist, he puts on the image of a man. His office is to discover the virtues of birds and precious stones, and to make the similitude of all kinds of birds to fly before the Exorcist, singing and drinking as natural birds do. He governs 30 Legions of Spirits.

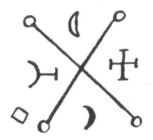

$\mathfrak{S}$EERE

PRINCE
1°—10° Pisces (night)
February 19—28

EIGHT OF CUPS   JUPITER—TIN

$\mathfrak{T}$he Seventieth Spirit is Seere, Sear, or Seir. He is a Mighty Prince, and powerful, under AMAYMON, King of the East. He appears in the form of a beautiful man, riding upon a winged horse. His office is to go and come; and to bring abundance of things to pass on a sudden, and to carry or re-carry anything wherever you would have it go, or where you would have it from. He can pass over the whole Earth in the twinkling of an Eye. He gives a true relation of all sorts of theft, and of hidden treasure, and of many other things. He is of an indifferent good nature, and is willing to do anything which the Exorcist desires. He governs 26 Legions of Spirits.

𝔇ANTALION

DUKE
10°—20° Pisces (night)
March 1—10

NINE OF CUPS   VENUS—COPPER

𝕿he Seventy-first Spirit is Dantalion. He/she is a Great and Mighty Duke, appearing in the form of a man with many countenances, all men's and women's faces; and he/she has a book in his/her right hand. His/her Office is to teach all Arts and Sciences unto any; and to declare the Secret Counsels of any one; for he/she knows the thoughts of all men and women, and can change them at will. He/she can cause love, and show the likeness of any person anywhere in the world. He/she governs 36 Legions of Spirits.

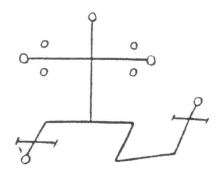

ANDROMALIUS

EARL
20°—30° Pisces (night)
March 11—20

TEN OF CUPS   MARS—IRON

The Seventy-second Spirit in order is named Andromalius. He is an Earl, great and mighty, appearing in the form of a man holding a great serpent in his hand. His office is to bring back both a thief, and the stolen goods; to discover all wickedness, and underhanded dealings; and to punish all thieves and other wicked people; and also to discover hidden treasures. He rules over 36 Legions of Spirits.

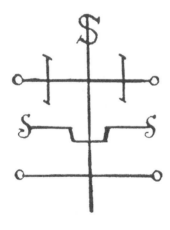

CHAPTER NINE

Goetia Evocation and Psychological Types

We have already discussed the psychological and non-psychological aspects of the Goetic Spirits. The disciplined use of these Spirits can bring about significant psycho-spiritual changes not unlike those achieved by psychotherapy.

As interesting and effective as your evocations can be they are more useful if you can discover which Spirits operate in your life independent of your will and which ones you should evoke in order to enrich and balance your life.

For example Spirit number 12 SITRI (attributed to the 3rd Decan of Cancer and to the 4 of Cups) for the daytime and HAAGENTI number 48 (4 Cups) for the night are the Spirits which operate for me. My birthday is July the 12th. These two Spirits govern beauty, lust, wisdom and gold. The night vision is involved with alchemy and wisdom which are two major topics that have always interested me. The day vision is lust and beauty which are also powerful forces in my life. Combining these visions we have the Great Occult secret, the alchemical process of transmuting the body through lust into gold. This is, of course, associated with Sex Magick.

In addition to the obvious associations between date of birth and the Goetia Spirits there are many other Goetic forces which manifest themselves in our lives. By knowing these forces you can evoke them and integrate them within your psyche. If for example you are susceptible to wild moods or outbursts or if you often feel weak try to find the appropriate Spirit and evoke it. Begin a "relationship" or dialogue with the Spirit. Ask it what it is trying to communicate to you. Command it to cease affecting you or reward it depending on what you are trying to accomplish.

Keep in mind that reward and punishment are two of the primary means of communicating with Goetia Spirits. Sometimes, instead of direct punishment withholding something the Spirit wants works will. The important thing to keep in mind is that your operation must be under *your Will*. Capricious behavior will not benefit you. Plan out your operations carefully.

TYPES OF PEOPLE AND TYPES OF SPIRITS

A simple understanding of psychological types as laid down by Carl Jung will be very useful in your workings.

While I am not an advocate of his therapy or that of his followers, I am very respectful of his genius and the maps of the mind he has given us.

The first major type is the extravert. For the extravert energy flows from him to the outside world while in his unconscious mind he is pushing the outside world away from him.

The second major type is the introvert. He feels overwhelmed by the outside world and wishes to push it away from him. On the other hand he is fed by the outside world and secretly invests his own energy into it which in turn also overwhelms him.

The introvert is interested in "banishing objects," that is removing their effect upon him, while the extravert is particularly interested in evoking objects or bringing them closer to him. In Goetia evocation the introvert might practice a more extraverted form, while the extrovert might try a more introverted form of evocation.

Goetia evocations can also be related to time. Day time evocations are more extroverted and less frightening, while night time evocations are more introverted and more frightening. Certain Spirits can be more in harmony with extraversion while others more in harmony with introversion.

Or it might be time to explore a repressed function by evoking Spirits which are opposite of the conscious attitude. For example, introverts might evoke extraverted Spirits at night while extraverts might evoke introverted Spirits during the day.

Throughout the life of a person a proper balance can occur when the extravert learns introversion and the introvert learns extraversion. Frequently this balance occurs by making the opposite point of view conscious and in the case of evocation "visible" in the form of a particular Spirit. In drawing the sigil and evoking the Goetic figures which represent the opposite of your conscious attitude you will begin to know and gain control of the repressed parts of your personality.

In addition to the two major types which Jung speaks about there are four other functions—two known as the "rational" functions (thinking and feeling) and two known as the "irrational" functions (sensation and intuition).

These four functions or types also represent approaches to life. The "opposite" or inferior (less used) function for the thinking type is feeling and *vice versa.* The "opposite" or inferior function for the sensation type is intuition and *vice versa.* Most of us tend to favor our strong "suit" while neglecting our inferior "suit." Confronting your weaker function can be very unpleasant, thus people have a tendency to project on others the dark side of their weaker function. In some cases friendships are based on two individuals each having the opposite of their inferior function as the other's superior function.

This can serve the person by keeping his weaker or less developed component out of consciousness or awareness. It can also lead to many problems. Evocation can be used to develop the weaker or inferior function.

Knowing how to identify the various types will also help the operator choose the correct partner in operations where mediumship is essential. Certain types do not make good mediums for the manifestation of particular Spirits. One reason for failure in Goetia workings is that people do not spend enough time examining the issues of types and personalities.

Now the question arises as why should one develop one's inferior function? This is a sensible question and without falling into the moralistic trappings of Jung or his followers I will simply say because it is a Gold Mine. The dross or the weaker function is rich in symbolic material and energy and provides the person with qualities and abilities missing in his life. Without having to embellish further, developing the inferior function makes you feel better. Notice I did not say more whole. You can't know wholeness except possibly by feeling better. Wholeness is an abstraction, feeling better is not.

The psychological model of types provides the operator with an excellent opportunity to explore Goetia from a different point of view and with a different aim in mind. This is not to say that evocation should be practiced solely for these purposes.

Evocation is a result oriented operation. It is not "High Magick" with sublime altruistic aims. It is practical and down to earth, designed to "get answers" and cause effects.

CHAPTER TEN

TRanCing OuT aNd SeXuAL EcStaSy
Goetia Evocation and The Orgasm of Death

T he breaking of expectation is one of the best means of going into Trance. If you observe yourself closely you will note how the above phrase affected you. The mixing of capital letters with small letters in an unexpected way disrupts the "set" of the mind. The mind desires to escape from this disruption by trance. Now read on and see when you begin to *slip* into TRanCe.

You couldn't miss it even if you tried, yet you might have forgotten the effect already. *Remembering* how to forget or forgetting how to *remember* is very important in learning how to trance. Now read these sentences again, very slowly but with an outer sense of silence. Do it again, Now!

As you repeat this operation you will begin to notice certain things happening. Some of these things will be very new and others you are already well familiar with. Try it again. This time do it loudly. When you are ready just let go.

Light two candles and place them next to a mirror. Stare into the mirror. You will be the medium and the operator will make passionate love to you. This is your chance to be completely free. The operator is in charge. You are there simply to receive.

You will enjoy letting go deeper and deeper into EcStAsy. Do not tense your body until you are ready. There is no reason to do anything until you are ready. Think a moment, feel *it* touch you, and let go. See the image, watch it change, bit by bit, and begin to feel the whirlings surround you. Now relax a bit more, but not before you tense your body one last time. Be sure to tense your entire body with style. Stretch.

The operator should have performed all the necessary preliminaries. Before you go deeper ask him if everything is prepared for you. Once you know that the circle is made, whatever is left can begin to leave you. You will become the open receptacle to be filled by the Spirit of your choice. *Remember* everything should have been agreed upon ahead of time. Be alert to that Now—let go at once. Read the previous sentence one last time.

Move to the bed. This is your circle of safety and joy.

As passion overwhelms you let it go deeper and deeper. Open up! Become empty—wider and wider—feeling nothing, but melt with the vision—You are safe.

Let everything fill you, sense the joy as it changes from pain to pleasure. Feel it build a little and then let go. Become bigger and bigger, let more into you. Open up—wider and wider— Now. Yell, or scream if you wish or remain as silent as you are open.

Merge with your ecstasy. Feel no difference between yourself and what is going deeper into......*trust completely*. Don't stop. Let the sounds of the Spirit speak.

YOUR SEXUAL TRANCE

The above sexual trance can be modified to fit your own specific needs and abilities. It is important to allow yourself to go as deep as you can. You should read the above example a couple of times before actually starting the procedure. Get a sense of the excitement. Feel free to design and redesign your sexual trance until it suits your needs.

The use of sex and hypnosis in Goetia evocation is unique to this particular book, that is not to say that others have not attempted these experiments and reported them in other writings. What we are doing here is dealing openly with the issue and providing a workable framework. Remember our framework is not made of stone and appropriate alterations can be made with experience.

We have found that the combination of sex and hypnosis is ideal in expanding the reception of the Medium providing more profound and interesting data from the Spirit. However, it should be pointed out that this operation should not be undertaken unless both the operator and the medium have agreed openly to undertake it and have spelled out all the details. This working requires special preparation and thus both participants should work out the details together well before they start their workings. The medium should know ahead of time that the operator will sexually exhaust the medium. This is essential for the best results. Sometimes there may be some minor discomfort for the medium in this part of the operation and the medium should allow the discomfort to dissipate at its own accord. The operator should be aware that he is manipulating high energy charges and should be very sensitive to the minor discomforts as indications that a new level of ecstasy is about to occur.

SOME THOUGHTS TO KEEP IN MIND

The sexual trance is ideal for working with emotional dislikes or revulsions to particular Spirits or their Seals. It is also an ideal way of working with relationship issues as well as dealing with repressed subconscious material.

The Medium might look at a skrying mirror (mentioned earlier) to enhance visual imagery. It can be placed on the ceiling or the floor outside of the circle. Be sure to put the skrying mirror in a triangle.

When the Spirit appears, the operator intensifies sexual activity, but not so much as to distract from the vision. The operator should have a sense of when to ask questions and must take complete charge in directing the session. The person who is acting as the Medium must feel completely free to let go. The Medium should not feel responsible for the outcome of the session.

Pains should be taken to be aware of all the Goetia rules before starting this operation. The license to depart could coincide with an orgasm. The operator should be certain that the Medium has snapped out of the trance once the session is over.

APPENDIX

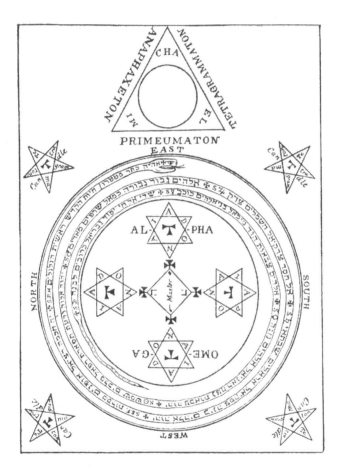

Traditional Circle

Modern Circle

Hexagram of Solomon

Pentagram of Solomon

Magical Ring

Sun & Moon Conjoined

Signs of the Grades

Shu

Set

Auramot

Thoum-aesh-
neith

Signs of the Grades (continued)

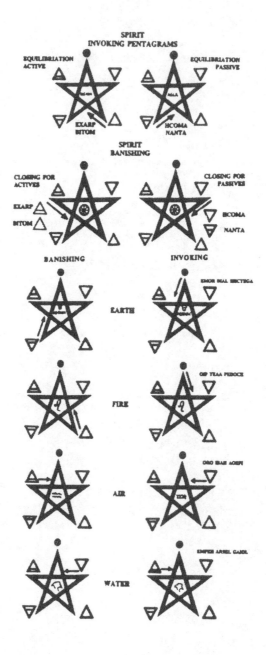

THE LESSER BANISHING RITUAL OF THE PENTAGRAM

THE QABALISTIC CROSS

Face East:

Touch your Forehead and say **Atoh (ah-toh)**
Touch your Heart and say **Malkuth (mal-kooth)**
Touch your Right Shoulder and say **Ve-Geburah (veh-gee-boo-rah)**
Touch your Left Shoulder and say **Ve-Gedulah (veh-gee-doo-lah)**
Touch your Heart and say **Le-Olam (lee-oh-lum)**
Point the symbolic dagger inward and say **Amen (ah-mayn)**

BANISHING

With your arm extended and still facing East:

Trace the Banishing pentagram of Earth, and vibrate **YHVH (yoad-hay-vaahv-hay)** as you thrust your symbolic dagger into the heart of the pentagram.

With your arm still extended, turn to the South:

Trace the Banishing pentagram of Earth and vibrate the name **ADONAI (ah-do-noy)** as you thrust your symbolic dagger into the heart of the pentagram.

With your arm still extended, turn to the West:

Trace the Banishing pentagram of Earth and vibrate the name **EHIEH (eh-hay-yay)** as you thrust your symbolic dagger into the heart of the pentagram.

With your arm still extended, turn to the North:

Trace the Banishing pentagram of Earth and vibrate the name **AGLA (ah-guh-lah)** as you thrust your symbolic dagger into the heart of the pentagram.

With your arm still extended, return to the East, completing the circle. Now imagine yourself surrounded in a Flaming Circle of four Pentagrams.

Stand straight with your arms out, forming the shape of a Cross:

Say:

Before me **Raphael (rah-fay-ale)**
Behind me **Gabriel (gah-bree-ale)**
At my right shoulder, **Michael (mee-ki-ale)**
At my left shoulder, **Auriel (oh-ree-ale)**

Then say:

Before me **flames the Pentagram**
Behind me **shines the six-rayed star**

COMPLETION

Finish by repeating the Qabalistic Cross:

Touch your Forehead and say **Atoh (ah-toh)**
Touch your Heart and say **Malkuth (mal-kooth)**
Touch your Right Shoulder and say **Ve-Geburah (veh-gee-boo-rah)**
Touch your Left Shoulder and say **Ve-Gedulah (veh-gee-doo-lah)**
Touch your Heart and say **Le-Olam (lee-oh-lum)**
Point the symbolic dagger inward and say **Amen (ah-mayn)**

FROM CHRISTOPHER S. HYATT, Ph.D.

THE PSYCHOPATH'S BIBLE

Throughout time, psychopaths have gotten a bad rap. That is quite understandable since almost all of the world's religious and social philosophies have little use for the individual except as a tool to be placed in service to their notion of something else: "God," or the "collective," or the "higher good" or some other equally undefinable term. Here, finally, is a book which celebrates, encourages and educates the best part of ourselves — The Psychopath.

TO LIE IS HUMAN

Not Getting Caught Is Divine

Introduced by Robert Anton Wilson

Take a tour of the prison erected by the lies that society tells you...and the lies you tell yourself. Then, learn the tools to tunnel out...

"Is it possible to use language to undo the hallucinations created by language? ...a few heroic efforts seem able to jolt readers awake... to transcend words."
— Robert Anton Wilson

FROM CHRISTOPHER S. HYATT, Pн.D.

THE ENOCHIAN WORLD OF ALEISTER CROWLEY
Enochian Sex Magick

*With Aleister Crowley &
Lon Milo DuQuette*

Many consider Enochiana the most powerful and least understood system of Western Occult practice. For the first time this esoteric subject is made truly accessible and easy to understand. Includes an Enochian dictionary, extensive illustrations and detailed instructions for the integration of Enochiana with Sex Magick.

PACTS WITH THE DEVIL
A Chronicle of Sex, Blasphemy & Liberation

With S. Jason Black

Braving the new Witchcraft Panic that is sweeping America, *Pacts With The Devil* places the Western magical tradition and the Western psyche in perspective. Contains a detailed history of European 'Black Magic' and includes new editions of 17th and 18th century Grimoires with detailed instruction for their use. Extensively illustrated.

FROM CHRISTOPHER S. HYATT, PH.D.

RADICAL UNDOING
The Complete Course for Undoing Yourself

For the first time on DVD, these effective and powerful Tantric methods help you to open your Chakras and release your Kundalini energy. With practice you will learn to harness this powerful sexual energy and experience *The Ultimate Orgasm*.

ENERGIZED HYPNOSIS

With Calvin Iwema, M.A.

Energized Hypnosis is a *breakthrough* program of DVDs, CDs, booklets and a "non-book" for gaining personal power, peace of mind and enlightenment. The techniques of **Energized Hypnosis** were developed many years ago by Dr. Christopher Hyatt and Dr. Israel Regardie, but have remained "in the closet"...until now.

THE *Original* FALCON PRESS

Invites You to Visit Our Website:
http://originalfalcon.com

At our website you can:

- Browse the online catalog of all of our great titles
- Find out what's available and what's out of stock
- Get special discounts
- Order our titles through our secure online server
- Find products not available anywhere else including:
    – One of a kind and limited availability products
    – Special packages
    – Special pricing
- Get free gifts
- Join our email list for advance notice of New Releases and Special Offers
- Find out about book signings and author events
- Send email to our authors
- Read excerpts of many of our titles
- Find links to our authors' websites
- Discover links to other weird and wonderful sites
- And much, much more

Get online today at http://originalfalcon.com

Made in the USA
San Bernardino, CA
27 September 2018